George C Hugg, Frank L Armstrong

Crowning Triumph

a new collection of sacred songs and gospel hymns, for sanctuary,

Sunday-schools, prayer and praise meetings, the home circle,

anniversaries, funeral occasions, etc.

George C Hugg, Frank L Armstrong

Crowning Triumph
a new collection of sacred songs and gospel hymns, for sanctuary, Sunday-schools, prayer and praise meetings, the home circle, anniversaries, funeral occasions, etc.

ISBN/EAN: 9783337270476

Printed in Europe, USA, Canada, Australia, Japan

Cover: Foto ©Andreas Hilbeck / pixelio.de

More available books at **www.hansebooks.com**

The Crowning Triumph

A

NEW COLLECTION

OF

Sacred Songs and Gospel Hymns.

FOR

*SANCTUARY, SUNDAY-SCHOOLS, PRAYER AND
PRAISE MEETINGS, THE HOME CIRCLE.
ANNIVERSARIES, FUNERAL
OCCASIONS, ETC.*

By GEORGE C. HUGG & FRANK L. ARMSTRONG

PHILADELPHIA:

F. A. NORTH & CO.

1308 Chestnut Street.

DEALERS IN SHEET MUSIC, MUSIC BOOKS, MUSICAL INSTRUMENTS,
AND ALL KINDS OF MUSICAL MERCHANDISE.

J. M. ARMSTRONG & Co., Music Typographers, Philadelphia.

Prefatory.

WHILE the numerous compositions embraced herein must speak separately for themselves, it is believed that the collection will be found to possess an unusual number of the requisites of excellence, and variety sufficient to suit all tastes and capacities. The hope is indulged that it will tend to promote the science of vocal music in the Sunday-school and the family circle, and prove acceptable to the religious community.

GEORGE C. HUGG,
FRANK L. ARMSTRONG.

SPECIAL NOTICE TO SUNDAY-SCHOOL COMMITTEES, AND OTHERS.

☞ *Any person printing the copyright words or music contained in this book, without the written permission of the publishers, will be held amenable to the copyright law, which imposes a fine of one dollar for each copy so printed.* ☜

THE PUBLISHERS.

THE CROWNING TRIUMPH

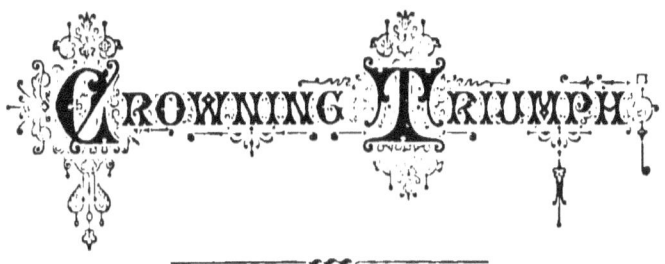

Hymn of Praise.

ADAM GEIBEL.

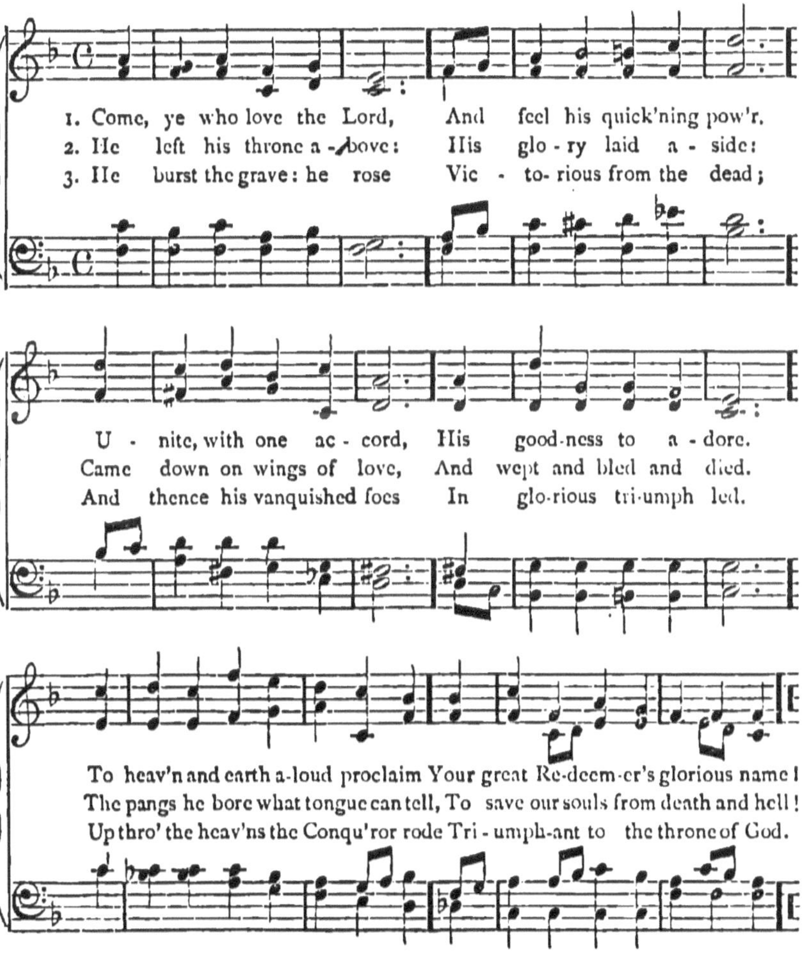
1. Come, ye who love the Lord, And feel his quick'ning pow'r.
2. He left his throne a - bove: His glo - ry laid a - side:
3. He burst the grave: he rose Vic - to- rious from the dead;
U - nite, with one ac - cord, His good-ness to a - dore.
Came down on wings of love, And wept and bled and died.
And thence his vanquished foes In glo-rious tri-umph led.
To heav'n and earth a-loud proclaim Your great Re-deem-er's glorious name!
The pangs he bore what tongue can tell, To save our souls from death and hell!
Up thro' the heav'ns the Conqu'ror rode Tri - umph-ant to the throne of God.

Waiting for Jesus.

Waiting for the coming of our Lord Jesus Christ.—1 Cor., i, 7.

M. E. SERVOSS.   GEO. C. HUGG.

With feeling.

1. Waiting for Je - sus, and working while I wait;   His lab'-rers they are
2. Waiting for Je - sus, and working while I wait;   Sow-ing on hill and
3. Waiting for Je - sus, and working while I wait; What though the hours seem

few, they are few,   So I will work with an earn-est, lov-ing heart, And
plain; hill and plain; Reap-ing with care all the fruit of earn-est toil, A
long; hours seem long; Great - er the har - vest I then may garner in, And

hands that are kind   and   true.
har - vest of gold - en   grain.   Wait-ing for Je - sus, And
sweet - er the har - vest - song.

CHORUS.

working while I wait; Sure-ly my heart is blest; Waiting for Je - sus, and

working while I wait, And then go - ing home to rest.

FANNY CHADWICK.

F. L. ARMSTRONG.

With energy.

1. Oh, wide sweep the wa-ters of life's roll-ing sea, And strong are the
2. When Peace spreads her pinions a - broad o'er the wave, And hush'd are the
3. All fear-less we ride o'er the bil-lows' mad foam. The Lord is our

storm-winds, un - brok-en and free; Mid gloom and mid per - il, out-
tem-pests, no long - er to rave, With grate-ful thanks-giv-ing of
Pi - lot, to guide us safe home: Through sunlight and shad - ow He

-rings our loud cry, Save, Lord, or we per-ish! Oh, hear us on high!
soul and of voice, To Him who hath saved us, we'll ev - er re - joice.
rul - eth the gale: Our hope is an An-chor that nev-er can fail.

CHORUS.

O Lord of life's sea,   we call un-to thee: A - rise in thy

Lord of life's sea   call un-to thee.

mercy, dear Lord of life's sea, A -rise in thy mer-cy, dear Lord of life's sea.

6. Singing on the Way.

"The ransomed of the Lord shall return, and come to Zion with songs."—ISA. XXXV. 10.

M. E. SERVOSS. JNO. R. SWENEY.

1. We will sweet-ly sing on the gold-en shore, Where all is joy and gladness; Forevermore with Christ we'll reign, Released from care and sadness.

2. We are sure our Fa-ther knows all our need, Each heartache, pain, and sor-row; So in His hands we'll leave it all, And trust Him for the mor-row.

3. We will sing of Je - sus, our Sa-viour-King, Whose wondrous love is o'er us; Who guides our footsteps, lest they stray, And makes all plain before us.

CHORUS.

Then a - long the way, the Lord's highway, With voi-ces clear and ring - ing, We'll shout hosan-na as we go, And en-ter Zi - on sing - ing.

4.
We will sing of heaven,—our nome above,
With all its joy and glory;
And to the world, where'er we go,
We'll tell salvation's story.

Going up to Zion.

And the ransomed of the Lord shall return, and come to Zion with songs and everlasting joy upon their heads.—ISAIAH, XXXV, 10.

A. S. DOUGHTY. · GEO. C. HUGG.

1. On-ward, pil-grim, don't de - lay; Go re-joic-ing on the way
2. In the way mark'd out of old, Fol - low line of du - ty bold;
3. Each step for-ward, up or down, Met by scorn, re - buke, or frown,

Ris - ing high-er ev' - ry day, While trav'ling up to Zi - on.
Then each dan - ger you be - hold, Will prove a chain-ed li - on.
Brings us near - er to the crown We shall re - ceive in Zi - on.

CHORUS.

Go-ing up high-er, go-ing up high-er, High-er up to Zi - on;

Go-ing up high-er, high-er, high-er, To the cit - y of our God.

4 Sorrows and afflictions meet;
Dangers threaten, trials greet;
Fear not! Jesus guides the feet,
And points the way to Zion.—*Chorus.*

5 On the mount His praise prolong;
Pass the gloomy vale with song;
Richest blessings ever throng
The pilgrim's way to Zion.—*Chorus.*

In Jesus.

For in Thee, O Lord, do I hope.—PSALM xxxviii, 15.

M. E. SERVOSS.

ADAM GEIBEL.

1. Hoping in Je - sus, hoping in Je - sus, He is my
2. Trusting in Je - sus, trusting in Je - sus, He is my

Sav - iour, He is my all; Hoping in Je - sus, hoping in
Rock, my Ref - uge, my Rest; Trusting in Je - sus, trust-ing in

Je - sus, Will you not come when you hear His sweet call? See He is
Je - sus, Ye who will trust Him shall ev - er be blest Will you not

waiting; hark! he is call - ing, "Come unto Me," all ye weary ones, come."
seek Him? will you not love him? Je-sus the Sav - iour who died for your sin.

Lean on His arm, and He will pro - tect thee, Guide thee through
Knock at the door, it quick-ly will op - en, And Je - sus

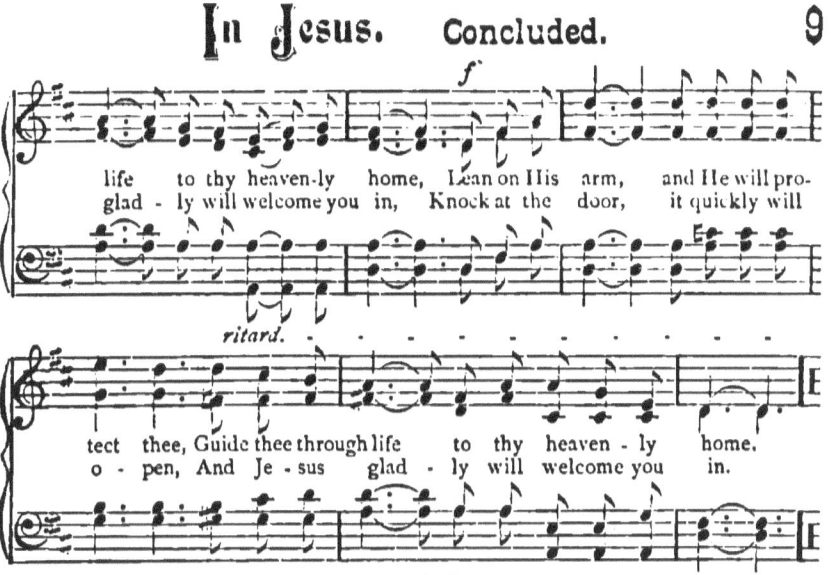

life   to thy heaven-ly   home, Lean on His   arm,   and He will pro-
glad - ly will welcome you in,   Knock at the   door,   it quickly will

tect thee, Guide thee through life   to thy heaven - ly   home.
o - pen, And Je - sus   glad - ly will   welcome you   in.

3 Resting in Jesus, resting in Jesus,
   He is my Guide, my Shepherd my Life ;
   Resting in Jesus, resting in Jesus,
   You who would rest from your trouble and strife,
   Flee to Him now, and He will receive you,
   Rest in his love, and your guide He will be,
   Peace He will give to all who will ask it,
   Come to Him now, for His mercy is free.

Weber. 7s.

A broken and a contrite heart, O God, Thou wilt not despise.—PSALM, li, 17.

Rev. CHAS. WESLEY, 1740.   C. M. VON WEBER.

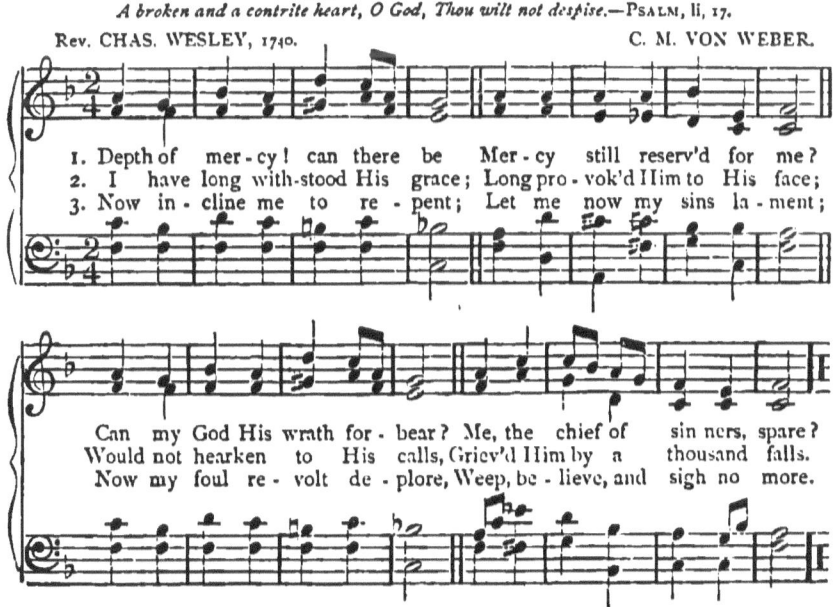

1. Depth of   mer - cy ! can there be   Mer - cy   still reserv'd for   me ?
2. I   have long with-stood His   grace; Long pro - vok'd Him to His   face;
3. Now in - cline me to   re - pent; Let me   now my   sins la - ment;

Can   my God His wrath for - bear ? Me, the   chief of   sin ners, spare ?
Would not hearken   to   His   calls, Griev'd Him by a   thousand falls.
Now my foul re - volt de - plore, Weep, be - lieve, and   sigh no   more.

10　The Rock's Blessed Shadow.

C. WESLEY.

GEO. C. HUGG.

1. Thou Rock of my sal-va-tion, haste,　Ex-tend Thine am-ple shade;
2. De-fend me in this try-ing hour;　My sure pro-tec-tion be;

And let it o-ver me be cast,　To screen my nak-ed head.
My shel-ter from the tempest's pow'r,　Till I am fixed on Thee.

CHORUS.

In the Rock's bless-ed shadow, I am rest-ing, resting, resting;

In the Rock's blessed shadow, I am resting; Sweetly resting in its shade.

3 O set upon Thyself my feet,
　And make me surely stand !
From fierce temptation's rage and heat,
　Protect me with Thy hand.—*Chorus.*

4 Now let me in the cleft be placed,
　Nor my defence remove ;
Within Thine arms of love embraced,
　Thine arms of endless love.—*Chorus.*

Who is He?

And it was the third hour, and they crucified Him.—MARK, xv. 25.

FOR EASTER.   F. L. ARMSTRONG.

Andante.

1. Bound up - on th'accursed tree, Faint and bleeding, who is He?
2. Bound up - on th'accursed tree, Sad and dy - ing, who is He?

See His eyes, so pale and dim; Streaming blood and writhing limb.
Hark! His pray'r for them that slew; "Lord, they know not what they do!"

See the flesh with scourges torn, See the crown of twist-ed thorn;
Lo, the sun at noon grown pale! Rent in twain the tem-ple's veil!

cres.   *rall.* - - - -

See the drooping death-dew'd brow; Son of man, 'tis Thou! 'tis Thou!
Trembling nature knows Thee now; Son of God, 'tis Thou! 'tis Thou!

3 Bound upon th'accursed tree,
  Dread and awful, who was He?
  Though His lifeless corpse was laid
  In a cold sepulchral bed,
  Soon the Saviour, from the grave,
  Rose, a conqueror strong, to save;
  Bright the crown that decks His brow:
  Son of God, 'tis Thou! 'tis Thou!

The Christian's Triumph.

O death, where is thy sting? O grave, where is thy victory?—1. Cor. xv. 55.

A. S. DOUGHTY.   GEO. C. HUGG.

Spirited.

1. Life's closing hours pass sweetly by, Earth's pains are felt no more;
2. With tri-als and with conflicts past, And re-cord placed on high,

To heav'n I now 'di - rect mine eye To view the shin-ing shore.
By faith I see the crown at last, And vict-'ry drawing nigh.

CHORUS.

Home - ward, home - ward, Home to the shin-ing shore;
On - ward, up - ward, we are marching,

Home - ward, home - ward, Home to the shin - ing shore.
On - ward, up - ward, we are marching.

3 The parting veil reveals the tide,
    Where on the margin wait
    My friends redeemed, the glorified,
    To sweep me through the gate.

4 As Nature sinks in Death's embrace,
    So will my spirit rise
    Triumphant through redeeming grace,
    To rest in Paradise.

Rejoice Evermore.

"Rejoice in the Lord always: and again I say, Rejoice." — PHIL. iv. 4.

M. E. SERVOSS.   ADAM GEIBEL.

1. Rejoice! rejoice! for Jesus reigns, The Prince of peace and love, To guide the chil-
2. Rejoice! rejoice! the Christ has come, The Saviour of mankind, To seek the lost ones
3. Rejoice! rejoice for - evermore, Nor let one soul repine. Though friends forget, and

dren of his grace To heav'n, their home above. And they who seek his loving care Thro'
of his fold, And heal the halt and blind. O   err - ing and re- pentant soul, Look
hearts grow cold, A Father's love is thine. And if the world seem dark with frowns, Just

dark and sunny days, Shall know how safely they may walk When God directs their ways.
up, and thou shalt live. The Friend of sinners comes to save, To ran-som and forgive.
meet them with a smile; And, with the hope of future bliss, All present ills beguile.

CHORUS.

Re-joice! re-joice for - ev - er - more! Im - man-uel's prais - es sing.

They must re-joice who sure - ly know That Je - sus is their King.

14 Press on, Veterans.

"I press toward the mark, for the prize of the high calling of God in Christ Jesus."—PHIL. iii. 14.

GEO. C. HUGG.

Spirited.

1. Press on, ye vet'- rans of the cross. Let
2. Press on, re - joic - ing as you go. Sing
3. Press on, tri - umph - ant far and near: The

faith in Christ your strength re - new! On to the new Je -
praise un - to your Lord and King; Whose might - y arm will
bat - tle fought, the vict' - ry won. The vic - tors rest, with-

ru - sa - lem, Where thy great Cap - tain waits for you.
lead you through; Whose love will sweet de - liv'- rance bring.
out one fear, In an e - ter - nal home of love.

CHORUS.

Ev - er press on, press on, press on! On to thy heaven-ly home;

Ev - er press on, press on, press on! On to thy heaven-ly home.

Rest Awhile.

"Come ye yourselves apart into a desert place and rest awhile."—MARK vi. 31.

E.

CHAS. EDW. POLLOCK.

1. In the green pastures of thy love, our Saviour, By the still wa - ters,
2. Care doth oppress and sorrow's shadow brood; Temp - ta tion beck - ons
3. Sa - viour, we rise and fol·low, at thy bidding, The path of du - ty, —
4. Bur - ied with thee we rise a·gain in pow'r; Thou for our sins for -

'neath thy gracious smile; Pray - ing, but trust - ing, then we pause to listen;
with se - duc·tive smile; But Lord, we come to thee in loving trust,
dark that path may be; We hear thy voice, "'Tis I, be not a - fraid!"
ev · er didst a - tone; Till at the last we hear thy joy·ful summons,

CHORUS.

Yes; thou art calling us to rest a - while.
For thou art calling us to rest a - while.
Whilst thou art calling us to rest with thee.
Come, rest for - ev - er in thy Fa - ther's home.

In the green pastures,

By the still wa-ters, 'Neath thy gracious smile; Pray-ing, but trusting,

Pause we to lis - ten, For thou art calling us to rest a - while.

Victory! Victory!

" Thanks be to God, who giveth us the victory through our Lord Jesus Christ."—I. Cor. xv. 37.

Dr. J. C. CURRAN.

GEO. C. HUGG.

March movement.

1. Pass a-long the war- cry, sol-diers of the Lord; Gird a-new your ar- mor, draw the trus - ty sword, March in ser- ried col - umn, shout- ing as you go,
2. Fierce the bat-tle ra - ges, dead- ly is the strife; But the prize a-waits you, "ev - er- last- ing life." Je - sus, your Command- er, gives you as you go,
3. Sa - tan's hosts are fly-ing, put to ut - ter rout; Hark! our valiant sol-diers raise their bat-tle-shout. Heav-en with the ech - o cheer- ful- ly resounds,

CHORUS.

Vic - to-ry! vic - to-ry! ov - er ev' - ry foe.
Vic - to-ry! vic - to-ry! ov - er ev' - ry foe. } Pass a-long the war- cry,
Vic - to-ry! vic - to-ry! ov - er ev' - ry foe.

Vic- to- ry! vic - to-ry! Pass a-long the war-cry, Vic- to- ry! vic - to- ry!

Pass along the war-cry, Shout it as you go, Victory! vic- tory! ov - er ev'-ry foe.

Make room for Jesus.

"And yet there is room."—LUKE xiv. 22.

Rev. ALEX. CLARK.   EASTBURN.

1. Make room for Je - sus! room, sad heart, Be-guiled and sick of sin;
2. Make room for Je - sus! room, make room! His hand is at the door;
3. Make room for Je - sus! soul of mine, He waits re-sponse to - day;

Bid ev - ry a - lien guest de-part. A - rise, and let him in.
He comes to ban - ish guilt and gloom, And bless thee more and more.
His smile is peace; his grace divine. Oh, turn him not a - way!

CHORUS.

Make room for Je - sus! by and by, Midst saint and ser - a - phim,

He'll welcome to his throne on high The souls that welcomed him.

4 Make room for Jesus! He will come,
    And loving grace bestow;
   And though thy sins as scarlet be,
    Will make them white as snow.—*Chorus.*

5 Make room for Jesus! let thy soul
    With tender love be rife.
   He'll guide and lead thee safely on
    To everlasting life.—*Chorus.*

Work for Jesus.

W. J. KIRKPATRICK.

Firmly.

1. In the name of God ad-van-cing, Sow thy seed at morn-ing light;
2. Look not to the far-off fu-ture; Do the work that near-est lies;

Cheer-i-ly the fur-rows turn-ing, La-bor on with all your might.
Sow thou must be-fore thou reap-est; Rest at last is la-bor's prize.

CHORUS.

Then work, work for Je-sus; Toil thro' the cloud or sun; Till the

Mas-ter bids thee rest From la-bor when thy work is all done.

3 Standing still is dangerous ever;
  Toil is meant for Christians now.
Let there be, when evening cometh,
  Honest sweat upon thy brow.

4 And the Master shall come smiling,
  At the setting of the sun,
Saying, as he pays the wages,
  "Good and faithful one, well done!"

As the Hart panteth.

"As the hart panteth after the water brooks, so panteth my soul after thee, O God."—Ps. xlii. 1.

GEO. C. HUGG.

1. As pants the hart for cool-ing streams, When heated in the
2. For thee, my God, the liv-ing God, My thirs-ty soul doth
3. Why rest-less, why cast down, my soul? Trust God, and he'll em-

chase, So longs my soul, O God, for thee, And thy re - fresh - ing grace.
pine; Oh, when shall I behold thy face, Thou Majes - ty Di - vine?
ploy His aid for thee, and change these sighs To thankful hymns of joy.

CHORUS.

As pants the hart for cool-ing streams,

As pants the hart for cool-ing

When heat - ed in the chase, So longs my soul,

streams; So longs my

Rit.

O God, for thee, And thy re - fresh - ing grace.

soul, O God, for Thee.

Rev. R. W. TOOD.   HARRY SANDERS. By per.

1. Oh, who is this that cometh From Edom's crimson plain, With wounded side, with
2. Oh, why is thine apparel With reeking gore all dyed, Like them that tread the

garments dyed? Oh, tell me now thy name. "I, that saw thy soul's distress, A
winepress red? Oh, why this bloody tide?   "I the winepress trod alone, 'Neath

ran - som gave.   I, that speak in righteousness, Mighty to save."
dark'n-ing skies.   Of the people there was none Mighty to save."

REFRAIN.

Might-y to save, . .   Might - y to save, . .

Might-y to save,   Might - y to save,

Mighty to save. Lord, I trust thy wondrous love, Mighty to save.

3. O bleeding Lamb, my Saviour,   I the bloody fight have won:
    How couldst thou bear this shame?   Conquered the grave.
"With mercy fraught, mine own arm   Now the year of joy has come,—
    Salvation in my name.   [brought   Mighty to save."

He Died for Me.

"While we were yet sinners, Christ died for us."—Rom. v. 8.

W. A. C.

WILBUR A. CHRISTY.

1. When the Mar-tyred One I see, Think of all His love for me,
2. Bless-ed One, hear Thou my cry; Weak and worth-less, Lord, am I;
3. When this heart is stilled to rest; When I rise to join the blest;

Love that suf-fered grief and shame, Crown of thorns and slandered name;
Noth-ing from Thy hand I claim; No ex-cuse my lips can frame;
When with that an-gel-ic throng, Shall these lips take up the song;

See His tears of an-guish flow, Shed for me, those tears I know,
Help me in Thy love to trust, Mer-ci-ful and good and just;
Though I sing my Saviour's praise, Through Eter-ni-ty's glad days,

This must still my won-der be, Did He die for such as me?
Though a won-der still it be, Thou didst die for such as me.
This for aye will won-der be, That He died for such as me.

CHORUS.

Did He die for such as me? Bleeding on the cru-el tree,
Did He die such as me, Bleeding on cru-el tree,

He died for Me. CONCLUDED.

rit.

Greater won - der cannot be Than that Je - sus died for me.
Greater won-der can-not, can-not be Than that Je-sus died for me.

Saved by Grace.

"By grace we are saved."—EPH. ii. 8.

W. A. O.

W. A. OGDEN, by per.

1. Sav'd by grace, oh, bless-ed tid - ings, Won-der - ful His love to show,
2. Sav'd by grace, oh, bless-ed tid - ings, Je - sus drank the cup for me,
3. Sav'd by grace, oh, bless-ed tid - ings, Hap - py he who can re - peat,
4. Sav'd by grace, I'll sing for - ev - er, Tell the wond-rous news a - broad,

Je - sus died to bring sal - va - tion To the per - ish - ing be - low.
Bow'd His head and cried "'Tis fin - ished!" Now my soul is count-ed free.
Who can sing redemption's sto - ry, Sit - ting at the Saviour's feet.
Spread the gos - pel tid - ings ev - er, "Wor-thy is the Lamb of God.

CHORUS.

Sav'd by grace, oh, bless - ed thought, By my Saviour's blood I'm bought.

Our Heavenly Home.

A. S. DOUGHTY.

F. L. ARMSTRONG.

Cheerfully.

1. A home in heav'n! what a bliss-ful thought, As we toil a-long in our wea-ry lot; With heart op-prest and by an-guish riv'n We look from earth to a home in heaven.

2. A home in heav'n, where we toil no more, But reign with Christ on the gold-en shore. In songs of praise we will there u-nite With the great throng ar-rayed in white.

3. Dear home in heav'n! may we all meet there; With the re-deemed all its glo-ry share; And with the an-gels a-round the throne For-ev-er dwell in that sweet, sweet home.

CHORUS.

Beau-ti-ful, beau-ti-ful home, Beau-ti-ful heav-en-ly home.

Beau-ti-ful, beau-ti-ful home, Waiting for me in the glo-ry-land.

On to Battle.

"Fight the good fight of faith."—1 Tim. vi. 12.

Dr. J. C. CURREAN.

GEO. C. HUGG.

Spirited.

1. Onward! Christian sol - diers, On-ward to the war.
2. Clad in roy - al ar - mor, O - ver- come the foe,
3. When the con-flict end - eth, When the bat - tle's done,

Hold the ban-ner firm - ly; Bat - tle for the Lord. Bear the cross of
Trus-ting in the Sa - viour As ye on-ward go. Sa tan's host doth
When the foe is vanquished, And the vic-t'ry won; Lay a side your

Je - sus As your standard high. Nev - er must ye wav - er;
fal - ter. See! they break and flee. For-ward! Chris-tian soldiers.
ar - mor, Put on robes of white. Then with Christ, your Master,

CHORUS.

Nev - er must ye fly.
On to vic - to - ry. Onward! Christian sol-diers, Vanquish ev'ry
Reign in end-less light.

foe: Trust-ing in the Sa-viour As ye on-ward go.

Sweetly rest in Thee.

" I will give you rest."—MATT. xi. 28.

A. S. DOUGHTY.

GEO. C. HUGG.

1. We shall sweetly rest in thee, O thou Lamb of Cal-va-ry! When our
2. When temp-ta-tions all are past, When no doubts our faith o'er-cast, When from
3. When all earthly prospects fail, When we've passed the gloomy vale; When from

sins are washed a-way, And our spir-its leave their clay.
sin for-ev-er free, We shall sweet-ly rest in thee.
all our sor-rows free, We shall sweet-ly rest in thee.

We shall rest, sweet-ly rest, We shall sweet-ly rest in thee.

We shall rest, sweetly rest.

CHORUS.

We shall sweet - - - ly rest in thee, O thou

We shall sweet - ly rest in thee, rest in thee!

Lamb of Cal-va-ry; When from all our sorrows

O thou Lamb of Cal-va-ry, dear to me: When from all our sorrows

free,   We shall sweet - - ly rest in thee.

free,   sor - rows free,   We shall sweet - ly rest in thee.

The Promise.

Mrs. P. MUNZINGER.   F. L. ARMSTRONG.
Andante.

1. As thy day thy strength shall be,   Is the promise giv - en thee
2. As thy day thy strength shall be. Think not what may happen thee!
3. Think'st thou he'll for - get his child Journeying through the dang'rous wild

By   thy Father,   God and Friend, Who re - lief will   ev - er send,
Leave   the fu - ture   in his care   Who guards all things ev' - ry-where,—
Of   this world's en-tang-ling snares, Toiling 'mid de - press - ing cares?

As   in humble   fer-vent prayer Thou dost all thy   need de - clare.
Guides   the earth up - on   its way   By His u - ni - ver - sal sway.
Ev' - ry day of   life thou'lt see   As thy day thy strength shall be.

Marching on.

THOS. H. FERGUSON.

1. We are marching on to reach that happy land. There we'll rest forever on the
2. Come, dear pilgrim, come: let none be left behind. Come and join in with us that the
3. It will not be long till we shall reach that shore. There we hope to meet with those who've

bright golden strand. There we all will join the heav'nly blood-washed band In
road you may find. For the Sa-viour leads us: he is good and kind. He'll
gone on be-fore. There we'll sit and sing with them for- ev - er- more Ho -

CHORUS.

singing praises to our Lord.
guide us to our hap-py home. } Then come and join us as we're marching, marching
san-nas to our God and King.

on, marching on, Then come and join us as we're
marching on, marching on,

march - ing. We will march and sing Hal - le - lu- jah Praise the Lord!

Ho, every one that thirsteth.

"Ho, every one that thirsteth, come ye to the waters."—ISA. lv. 1.

GEO. C. HUGG.

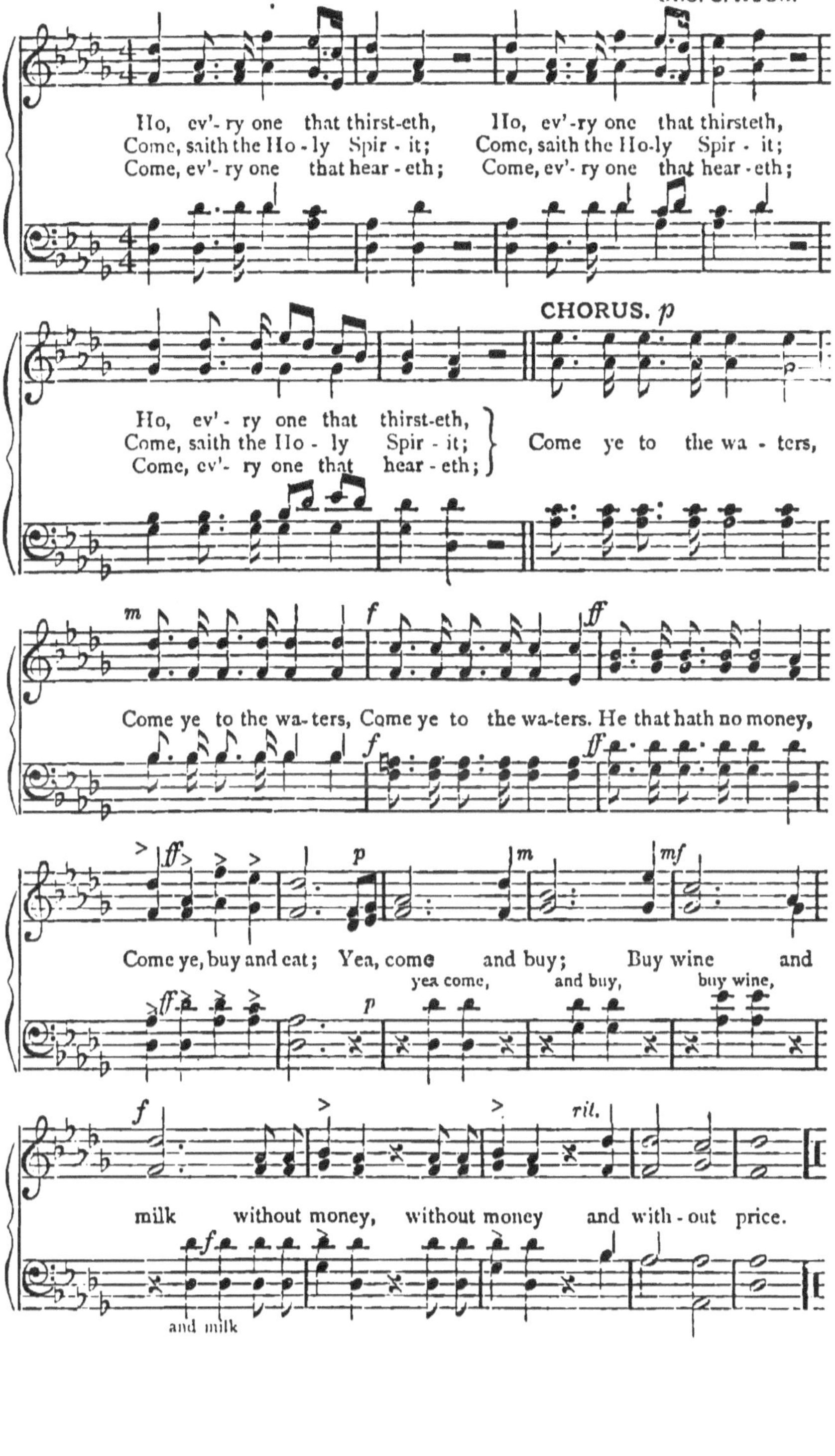

Ho, ev'-ry one that thirst-eth, Ho, ev'-ry one that thirsteth,
Come, saith the Ho-ly Spir-it; Come, saith the Ho-ly Spir-it;
Come, ev'-ry one that hear-eth; Come, ev'-ry one that hear-eth;
Ho, ev'-ry one that thirst-eth,
Come, saith the Ho-ly Spir-it;
Come, ev'-ry one that hear-eth;
CHORUS.
Come ye to the wa-ters,
Come ye to the wa-ters, Come ye to the wa-ters. He that hath no money,
Come ye, buy and eat; Yea, come and buy; Buy wine and
yea come, and buy, buy wine,
milk without money, without money and with-out price.
and milk
rit.

The Temperance Banner.

F. L. ARMSTRONG.

Spirited.

1. Un - furl the Temperance Ban - ner, And fling it to the breeze;
2. Come, join the no - ble ar - my; En - list now for the fight;
3. Then ral - ly round the stand - ard, And let the work go on

And let the glad ho - san - na Sweep ov - er land and seas. To
Main - tain our na - tion's hon - or; Firm stand ye for the right. Pro -
Un - til the last dim ves - tige Of in - tem - per-ance is gone. Be

God be all the glo - ry For what we now be - hold.
mote the cause of Temperance, To aid poor fal - len man;
earn - est in the bat - tle: Your weapons bold - ly wield.

Oh, let the cheering sto - ry In ev' - ry ear be told.
Put on the glorious ar - mor: Be fore-most in the van.
You'll sure - ly gain the vic - t'ry, And make the mon - ster yield.

C. WESLEY.   MENDELSSOHN.

1. Hark! the her - ald an - gels sing, "Glo - ry to the new-born King!
2. Mild he lays his glo - ry by; Born that man no more may die;

Peace on earth, and mer - cy mild, God and sin - ners rec - on-ciled."
Born to raise the sons of earth; Born to give them sec-ond birth.

Joy - ful, all ye nations, rise; Join the triumph of the skies:
Vail'd in flesh, the Godhead see, Hail th'incar - nate De - i - ty;

With th'angel - ic host proclaim, "Christ is born in Beth - le - hem."
Pleased as man with men t'ap-pear, Je - sus, our Im - man - uel, here.

Hark! the her - ald an - gels sing, Glo - ry to the new-born King.
Hark! the her - ald an - gels sing, Glo - ry to the new-born King.

The Children's Promise.

ALBERT MIDLANE.

With spirit.

ADAM GEIBEL.

1. There's a Friend for lit - tle chil - dren A - bove the bright blue sky, A
2. There's a rest for lit - tle chil - dren A - bove the bright blue sky, Who
3. There's a home for lit - tle chil - dren A - bove the bright blue sky, Where
4. There's a crown for lit - tle chil - dren A - bove the bright blue sky, And

Friend who never chang-es; Whose love will never die. Un-like our friends by
love the blessed Sa-viour, And to his Fa-ther cry; A rest from ev'- ry
Je - sus reigns in glo - ry, A home of peace and joy. No home on earth is
all who look to Je - sus Shall wear it by - and-by; A crown of brightest

nature, Who change with changeless fears, This friend is always worthy The
trou - ble, From sin and hun-ger free. There ev'-ry lit - tle pil-grim Shall
like it, Nor can with it com-pare; For ev'- ry one is hap-py, Nor
glo - ry, Which he shall sure bestow, On all who love the Saviour, And

precious name he bears. This friend is always worthy The precious name he bears.
rest e- ter-nal - ly. There ev'-ry lit - tle pil grim Shall rest e-ter-nal-ly.
can be happier there. For ev' - ry one is hap-py Nor can be happier there.
walk with him below. On all who love the Saviour, And walk with him below.

It wont be long.

A. S. KIEFFER. J. H. TENNEY.

1. Is thy young heart, O hap-py child, Now fill'd with youthful pleas-ure?
2. Is thy soul fill'd, in manhood's pride, With dreams of fame and glo-ry?
3. Is thy way dark, my broth-er dear? Does life to thee bring sor-row?

Look up from these, and ne'er for-get To place in heav'n thy treas-ure!
Look up from these and view the Cross, And read Redemption's sto-ry;
Look un-to him who guards thy life. Be-hold, there comes a mor-row!

It won't be long ere childhood days Have passed a-way for-ev-er.
It won't be long till life shall fade, Its lights go out for-ev-er.
It won't be long ere light shall dawn To gild thy life for-ev-er.

It won't be long ere childhood days Have passed away for - ev - er.
It won't be long till life shall fade, Its lights go out for - ev - er.
It won't be long ere light shall dawn, To gild thy life for - ev - er.

Then look be-yond, and see thy home Be-yond the rol-ling riv-er.
Oh, look be-yond, and view thy home Be-yond the rol-ling riv-er.
Look up to Him, be-hold thy home Be-yond the rol-ling riv-er.

4 It won't be long, it won't be long,
My sister and my brother;
Till life for us will all be past:—
Then let us love each other.
It won't be long till prayers and tears
Shall cease with us forever;
Oh, let us look to that sweet home
Beyond the shining river.

From "The Starry Crown," by permission.

34 Home over the River.

"Having a desire to depart."—Phil. i. 23.

A. S. DOUGHTY.

GEO. C. HUGG.

1. All our conflicts will here soon be end-ed, As pilgrims no longer we'll roam.
2. In that home we shall never hear sigh-ing; For sin nev-er tainted the air;
3. We shall dwell in the light of the glo - ry Of Him who once died to redeem;

In triumph we'll pass the dark riv - er, And join with our loved ones at home.
Nor feel the dread anguish of dy - ing; For all are im-mor-tal when there.
There oft we'll repeat the old sto - ry; And drink of the life-giv-ing stream.

CHORUS.

Our friends there will meet us at the river; They will greet us with a welcome on the

shore. With the angels we will view the golden city, And with saints we will dwell evermore.

4 We shall roam the blest fields near the river;
   And gaze on the glories displayed;
   Sing praise to the bountiful Giver;
   And feast 'neath the Tree of Life's shade.—*Chorus.*

5 When we're safe in that beautiful city,
   With friends and the loved ones of yore,
   The scenes of earth's sorrow and pity
   Will there be remembered no more.—*Chorus.*

JULIA WARD HOWE.   ADAM GEIBEL.

1. Mine   eyes have seen the   glo - ry Of   the   com-ing of the   Lord.
2. I have   seen him in   the watch-fire Of   a   hundred circling   camps.
3. I have   read   a   fi - ery   gos - pel Writ in   burnished rows of   steel:

He is   tramp - ling out   the   vin-tage Where the grapes of wrath are stored.
They have   build - ed him   an   al - tar In   the   ev'ning dews and damps.
As   ye   deal   with my con - temners, So   with   ye   my grace shall deal;

He   hath loosed the fa - tal   lightning Of his   ter - ri-ble swift sword. His
I   can read   his righteous sentence By   the   dim and flar - ing lamps. His
Let   the   he - ro born to   bat - tle Crush the   ser - pent with his heel, Since

truth   is marching on,   marching   on.   Marching   on,   marching
day   is marching on,   marching   on.   Marching   on,   marching
God   is marching on,   marching   on.   Marching   on,   marching

on, marching on, marching on,   His truth is marching on, marching on.
on, marching on, marching on,   His day   is marching on, marching on.
on, marching on, marching on,   Since God is marching on, marching on.

Onward, Christian Soldiers!

S. SULLIVAN.

1. On-ward, Christian sol - diers! marching as to war; With the cross of
2. Like a might - y ar - my moves the Church of God. Brothers, we are
3. Crowns and thrones may per-ish; kingdoms rise and wane; But the Church of
4. On-ward, then, ye peo - ple; join our happy throng. Blend with ours your

Je - sus go-ing on be - fore. Christ, the royal Master, leads against the foe.
treading where the saints have trod. We are not di-vi - ded: all one body we.
Je- sus constant will remain. Gates of hell can never 'gainst that Church prevail.
voi - ces in the triumph song. Glory, laud, and honor unto Christ the King.

CHORUS.

For-ward in - to bat - tle see, his ban-ners go.
One in hope and doc - trine: one in char - i - ty.
We have Christ's own prom - ise, and that can-not fail.
This thro' countless a - ges men and an-gels sing.

On-ward, Christian

sol - diers! Marching as to war; With the cross of Jesus go-ing on be-fore.

Song of Gladness.

J. R. SWENEY.

1. A song, a song of glad - ness!—For, though we here may part,
2. A - round thy throne of glo - ry, Blest Je - sus, an - gels sing!
3. Send us a part - ing bless - ing, O Fa - ther, from a - bove;

Breathe not a note of sad - ness; We still are joined in heart:
Tell - ing to all the sto - ry Of Christ, the Sa - viour - King:
May we, thy grace pos - sess - ing, Be saved to sing thy love,—

And long will we re - mem - ber This hap - py Sab-bath day,
'Tis this that tunes our voic - es This hap - py Sab-bath day,
And spend in heav'n for - ev - er A long and hap - py day!

And long will we re - mem - ber This hap - py Sab-bath day.
'Tis this that tunes our voic - es This hap - py Sab-bath day.
And spend in heav'n for - ev - er A long and hap - py day!

The Gospel Banner.

(MISSIONARY.)

J. A. GETZE.

1. Now be the gos-pel ban-ner In ev'-ry land un-
2. What though th'em-bat-tled le-gions Of earth and hell com-
3. Yes, thou shalt reign for - ev - er, O Je-sus, King of

furl'd; And be the shout, ho - san - na! Re-ech-oed through the world:
bine? His arm, throughout their re-gions, Shall soon re-splendent shine:
kings; Thy light, thy love, thy fa - vor, Each ransomed captive sings:

Till ev'-ry isle and na - tion, Till ev'-ry tribe and
Ride on, O Lord, vic-to - rious; Im-man-uel, Prince of
The isles for thee are wait - ing; The de-serts learn thy

ritard.

tongue, Re-ceive the great sal - va - tion, And join the hap-py throng.
peace: Thy triumph shall be glo - rious; Thy em-pire still in-crease.
praise; The hills and val-leys greet - ing, The song re-spon-sive raise.

The Great Teacher.

(FOR THE INFANT CLASS.)

F. L. ARMSTRONG.

Playfully.

1. I asked the lit-tle joy-ous bird who taught him how to fly,
2. I asked the lit-tle love-ly flow'r who gave her per-fume sweet,
3. I asked the lit-tle twink-ling star who taught him how to shine,

And sing such pret-ty lit-tle songs in the bright blue morning sky?
And dressed her in her vel-vet coat, so beau-ti-ful and neat?
And run with such a stead-y pace a - long his prop-er line?

And he told me it was God who had giv'n to him his wing,
And she told me it was God who had clothed her with such care,
And he told me it was God who had bid him shine so bright,

And taught him how to build his nest, and taught him how to sing.
And taught her how to breathe so sweet up - on the eve-ning air.
And trim his lit-tle ti - ny lamp to cheer the win - ter night.

4.

Since all things, then, look up to God,—the flower, the star, the bird,
And all obey his holy laws, and listen to his word;
I, too, although a child, will try his bidding to obey,
That I may learn to please him too, and serve as well as they.

40 Growing up for Jesus.

P. J. OWENS.   (INFANT CLASS.)   W. J. KIRKPATRICK.

1. Growing up for Je-sus, We are tru-ly blest. In his smile is welcome; In his
2. Not too young to love him, Little hearts beat true. Not too young to serve him As the
3. Growing up for Je-sus; Learning day by day How to fol-low onward In the

arms our rest. In his truth our treas-ure; In his love our rule.
dew-drops do. Not too young to praise him, Sing-ing as we come;
nar-row way. Seek-ing ho-ly treas-ure, Find-ing pre-cious truth;

CHORUS.

Growing up for Je-sus, In our Sun-day-school.
Not too young to answer When he calls us home. } Growing up for Je-sus,
Growing up for Je-sus In our hap-py youth.

Till in him complete; Growing up for Je-sus. Oh, his work is sweet

Growing up for Jesus, Till in him complete; Growing up for Jesus. Oh, his work is sweet.

Within thy Gates.

M. E. SERVOSS. GEO. C. HUGG.

1. With-in thy gates of peace, O ci-ty, fair to see,
2. Be-yond thy jas-per wall What glo-ry there a-waits
3. Up-on thy streets of gold Our toil-worn feet shall stand;
4. Free from each earth-ly wile Our feet no more shall roam;

Our feet from wand-'ring soon shall cease, And find a rest in thee.
For those who, at the Fa-ther's call, With joy approach thy gates!
Nor pleasures fade, nor joys grow old, With-in that peaceful land.
And, best of all, a Saviour's smile Will be our wel-come home.

CHORUS.

O jew-el-walled Je-ru-sa-lem! With pearly gates thrown wide,
thrown wide,

How glad-ly shall we en-ter in, And ev-er-more a-bide.

Unto the Hills.

M. E. SERVOSS.   JAS. R. MURRAY.

1. Un - to the shining hills of God, I lift my wea-ry eyes; And
2. Un - to the ev - er - last-ing hills, Crowned by the light of God, Un -
3. Un - to those light-crowned hills of love I press with earnest feet; And,

long to view the peaceful vales From whence those hills arise ; And when I think what
til, re-flecting down to earth, The narrow way seems broad; I look, when weary
looking upward to my goal, Earth's moments seem full fleet. 'Tis on- ly one brief

Organ.

glory waits For those who love God's ways, I gather strength for present need, And
of earth's toil, And by earth's snares alarmed. And, with my eyes upon those hills, I
life-time here: More zeal, my soul's request. So short a time to work for God: E -

CHORUS.

faith for future days. }
journey on unharmed. }   Unto the hills, the hills of God, I look with steadfast
ter - ni-ty to rest. }

gaze;   And gath- er strength for pres-ent need, And faith for future days.

More like Thee.

W. J. KIRKPATRICK.

1. Je-sus, Sa-viour, great Ex-am-ple, Pat-tern of all pu-ri-ty,
2. Lest I wan-der from thy path-way, Or my feet move wea-ri-ly,
3. When temptations fiercely low-er, And my shrinking soul would flee,

I would fol-low in thy footsteps, Dai-ly growing more like thee.
Sa-viour, take my hand and lead me. Keep me steadfast: more like thee.
Change each weakness in-to pow-er, Keep me spotless: more like thee.

CHORUS.

More like thee, more like thee. . Saviour, this my constant pray'r shall

More like thee, More like thee.

be, Day by day, where'er I stray, Make me more and more like thee.

4. When around me all is darkness,
    And thy beauties none may see,
  May thy beams, O Glorious Brightness,
    In effulgence shine through me.—*Cho.*

5 When death's cold, repulsive finger
    Leaves its impress on my brow,
  May thy life within me swelling,
    Keep me singing then as now.—*Cho.*

Be not afraid.

"Let not your heart be troubled."—John xiv. 1.

M. E. SERVOSS.

GEO. C. HUGG.

1. "Be not a-fraid!" 'twas Je-sus spoke. The wild waves fell a-sleep:
2. "Be not a-fraid," though clouds of wrong Almost obscure the right.
3. "Be not a-fraid" when death draws near; For death has lost its sting;

The ship that was by tem-pest tossed, Now rocked upon the deep; For
The voice that hushed the tem-pest's roar, Dis-pels life's dark-est night. The
And on the bor-ders of the grave The "birds of peace" may sing. Why

He with eyes di-vine had seen His chil-dren's toil and fear; And,
waves grow calm, the winds a-bate, The wa-ters gent-ly lave; The
should we fear when Je-sus calls From earth-ly toil and strife; To

CHORUS.

when the dark-est mo-ments came, The need-ed One drew near.
sea of life looks up and smiles When Je-sus walks its wave. } Be not a-
en-ter at his blest command, The pearl-y gates of life.

fraid! O heart, rejoice! O soul, be un-dis-
Be not a-fraid! O heart, re-joice! O soul, be un-dis-

cres.

mayed! A-bove life's fierc-est storm he speaks, 'Tis I! Be not a - fraid.

The Sabbath.

F. L. ARMSTRONG.

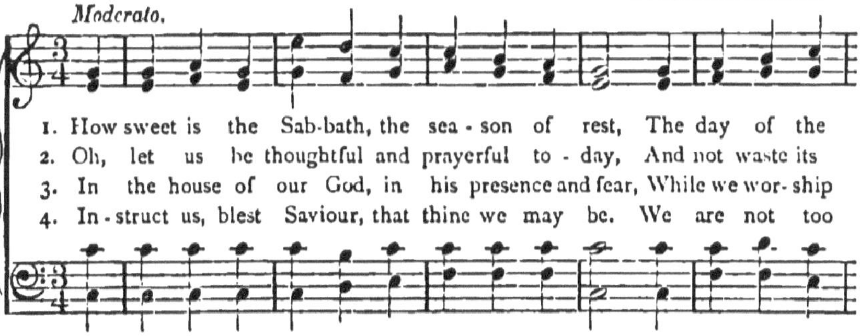

Moderato.

1. How sweet is the Sab-bath, the sea-son of rest, The day of the
2. Oh, let us be thoughtful and prayerful to - day, And not waste its
3. In the house of our God, in his presence and fear, While we wor-ship
4. In - struct us, blest Saviour, that thine we may be. We are not too

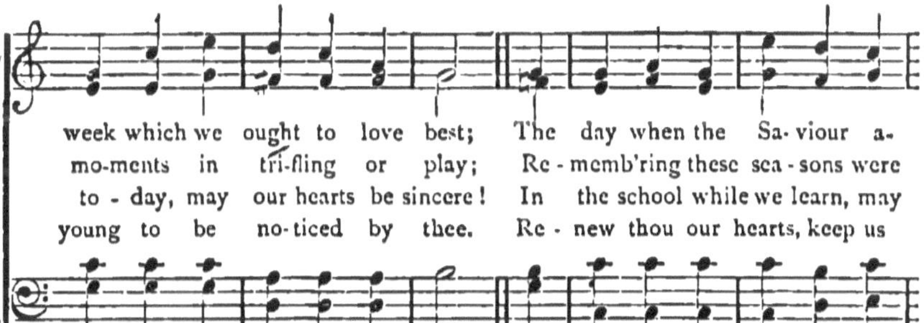

week which we ought to love best; The day when the Sa-viour a-
mo-ments in tri-fling or play; Re - mem'bring these sea - sons were
to - day, may our hearts be sincere! In the school while we learn, may
young to be no-ticed by thee. Re - new thou our hearts, keep us

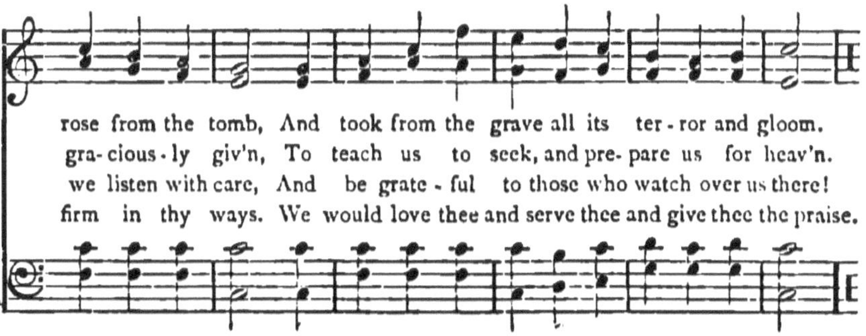

rose from the tomb, And took from the grave all its ter - ror and gloom.
gra-cious-ly giv'n, To teach us to seek, and pre- pare us for heav'n.
we listen with care, And be grate - ful to those who watch over us there!
firm in thy ways. We would love thee and serve thee and give thee the praise.

46 Singing with the Angels.*

E. A. HOFFMAN.

A. S. KIEFFER.

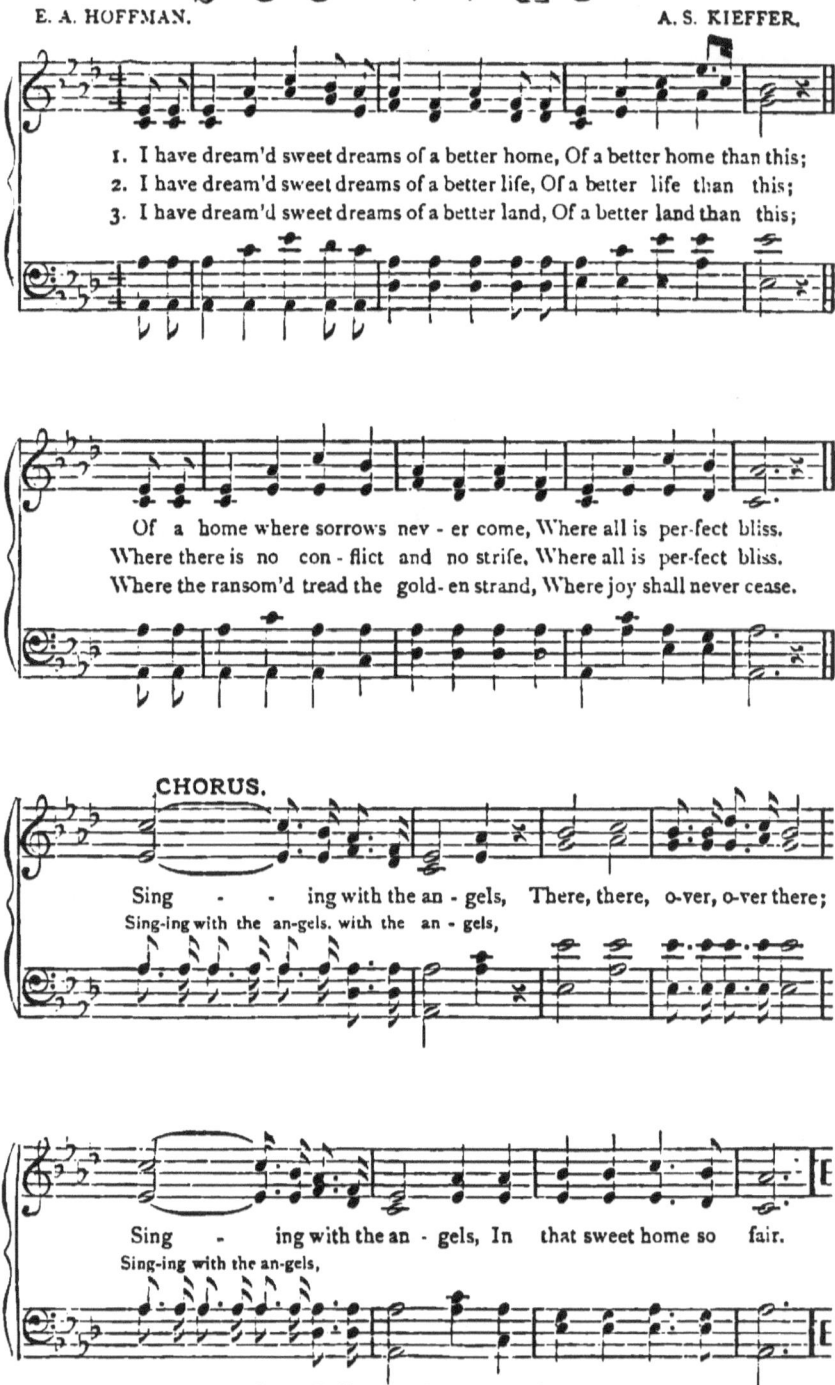

1. I have dream'd sweet dreams of a better home, Of a better home than this;
2. I have dream'd sweet dreams of a better life, Of a better life than this;
3. I have dream'd sweet dreams of a better land, Of a better land than this;

Of a home where sorrows nev - er come, Where all is per-fect bliss.
Where there is no con - flict and no strife, Where all is per-fect bliss.
Where the ransom'd tread the gold-en strand, Where joy shall never cease.

CHORUS.

Sing - - ing with the an - gels, There, there, o-ver, o-ver there;
Sing-ing with the an-gels. with the an - gels,

Sing - - ing with the an - gels, In that sweet home so fair.
Sing-ing with the an-gels,

*From " The New Starry Crown,' by permission.

M. F. SERVOSS.   ADAM GEIBEL.

1. Chil-dren of light, like the stars of the midnight,   Guiding earth's weary ones
2. Chil-dren of light, oh, how great is thy mission!   Shed ding abroad the bright
3. Chil-dren of light, till the day dawn appear eth,   God has commanded thee

home to their rest,   Shine for the heart that is burdened with anguish;
Gos-pel of truth!   Light ing the way to the glo-ry e-ter-nal!
ev-er to shine   All the long night till the brightness, God-given,

CHORUS.

Cheer up the lone-ly, the sad, and oppress'd.)
Guid-ing the a-ged: di-rect-ing the youth! }   Let thy light shine! for the
Los-eth its light in the glo-ry di-vine.)

world is in darkness. Hide not one ray, lest some prodigal child, Seek ing the

pathway to home and forgiveness, Groping in darkness, returns to the wild.

When the Spirit flies.

"Now we see through a glass darkly; then, face to face."—PAUL.

E. M. C.

E. MANFORD CLARK.

1. When the spir-it flies a-way, And the veil that in-tervenes Shall have
2. When the foot-prints by the way Where the wea-ry pil-grim trod Shall have
3. When the old has past a-way, And all things are made anew. In the

van-ished with the dawn of day; When this ten - ement of clay Shall have
fad - ed un-derneath the spray; When these fee - ble bod-ies lay 'Neath the
light of an immor-tal day; When the spir - it wends its way To the

done with earth-ly scenes, And with all of earth have gone its way;
cold and si - lent clod, And the spir - it seeks its home a - way;
realm of gold-en hue And the real man as - sumes the sway;

CHORUS.

Then shall we all know as we shall be known, And the Lord shall wipe all tears away;

Sor-row, pain and woe are for-ev-er flown When the spirit takes its flight a-way.

1. I'm a pil - grim and I'm a strang - er: I can tar-ry, I can tar-ry but a night. Do not de - tain me, for I am go - ing To where the fountains are ev - er flow - ing. I'm a pil - grim and I'm a stranger: I can tar-ry, I can tar - ry but a night.

2 There the glory is ever shining!
Oh, my longing heart, my longing heart is there.
Here in this country so dark and dreary,
I long have wandered forlorn and weary.

3 There's the city to which I journey:
My Redeemer, my Redeemer is its light!
There is no sorrow, nor any sighing,
Nor any tears there, nor any dying!

50 Pray without ceasing.

CHESTER E. POND.

1. My Lord and my Sa- viour, Cre - a - tor and King, Thy love and thy
2. If meet-ing with saints for com-mun- ion or pray'r, Or sing-ing a
3. If search-ing the Bi - ble for gems of its truth, Or teach-ing its

glo - ry for- ev - er I'll sing; My soul is in rap-tures: thou reignest within,
song with mel- o - di - ous air; If aid- ing the low- ly, the poor, or the weak,
pre-cepts to chil-dren or youth; If writ-ing for oth- ers on ho - li - est theme,

CHORUS.

To car- ry my burdens and cleanse me from sin. ⎞
Or urg-ing a sin- ner thy mer- cy to seek; ⎬ Oh, help me re-mem-ber, by
Or preaching the gospel their souls to re-deem; ⎠

night and by day, To "pray without ceasing," thy word to obey! For nothing will

rit.

cherish de - vo-tion in me Like se-cret and constant communion with thee.

The Advent.

(CAROL FOR INFANT CLASS.)

JENNIE JUNE.
Moderato.

KATIE SMITH.

1. Once in roy - al Da - vid's cit - y Stood a low - ly cat - tle-shed,
2. And our eyes at last shall see him, Through his own redeeming love;
3. Not in that poor, low - ly sta - ble, With the ox - en standing by,

Where a mo-ther laid her Ba - by In a man-ger for his bed:
For that Child, so dear and gen - tle, Is our Lord in heav'n a - bove;
We shall see him; but in heav-en, Set at God's right hand on high;

Ma - ry was that mo - ther mild, Je - sus Christ her lit - tle Child.
And he leads his chil-dren on To the place where he has gone.
When, like stars, his chil-dren crown'd, All in white, shall wait a - round.

CHORUS.

With the poor and mean and low - ly, Lived on earth our Sa-viour Ho-ly;

And he feel - eth for our sad-ness, And he shar-eth in our gladness.

Time and Eternity.

H. BONAR, D.D.   W. J. KIRKPATRICK.

Solo or Quartette.   *Chorus.*

1. It is not time that flies; 'Tis we, 'tis we are fly-ing. It
2. It is not truth that flies; 'Tis we, 'tis we are fly-ing. It
3. It is not hope that flies; 'Tis we, 'tis we are fly-ing. It
4. Yet we but die to live, It is from death we're fly-ing. For-

Solo or Quartette.   *Chorus.*

is not life that dies; 'Tis we, 'tis we are dy-ing.   Time and e-ter-ni-
is not faith that dies; 'Tis we, 'tis we are dy-ing.   O ev-er-during
is not hope that dies; 'Tis we, 'tis we are dy-ing.   Ye streams that have in
ev-er lives our life; For us there is no dy-ing: We die but as the

ty are one; Time is e-ter-ni-ty be-gun; Time changes, but with-
Faith and Truth, Whose youth is age, whose age is youth, Twin stars of im - mor-
heav'n your birth, Ye glide in gen-tle joy through earth; We fade like flow'rs be-
spring-time dies, In summer's golden joy to rise. These be our days of

out de-cay; 'Tis we a-lone who pass a-way.
tal-i-ty, Ye can-not per-ish from the sky.
side you sown,—Ye are still flow-ing, flow-ing on.
ver-nal bloom; Our har-vest is be-yond the tomb.

Brightly gleams our Banner. 53

T. J. POTTER. S. HENDERSON.

1. Bright - ly gleams our ban - ner, Pointing to the sky, Wav-ing wanderers
2. Je - sus, Lord, and Mas - ter, At thy sa - cred feet, Here with hearts re -
3. All our days di - rect us, In the way we go. Lead us on vic -
4. Then with saints and an - gels May we join a - bove, Offering end - less

on - ward To their home on high; Journeying o'er the de - sert,
joic - ing, See thy chil - dren meet; Oft - en have we left thee,
to - rious O - ver ev - ery foe; Bid thine an - gels shield us
prais - es At thy throne of love; When the toil is o - ver,

Glad - ly thus we pray, And with hearts u - ni - ted, Take our heav'nward way.
Oft - en gone a - stray; Keep us, migh - ty Sa - viour, In the nar - row way.
When the storm-cloud lower; Pardon thou and save us In the last dread hour.
Then comes rest and peace,—Je-sus, in his beau - ty;—Songs that nev-er cease.

CHORUS.

Bright - ly gleams our ban - ner, Point - ing to the sky,

rit.

Wav - ing wanderers on - ward To their homes on high.

Once More.

" I will sing of the mercies of the Lord forever."—Ps. lxxxix. 1.

J. E. H.

J. E. HALL.

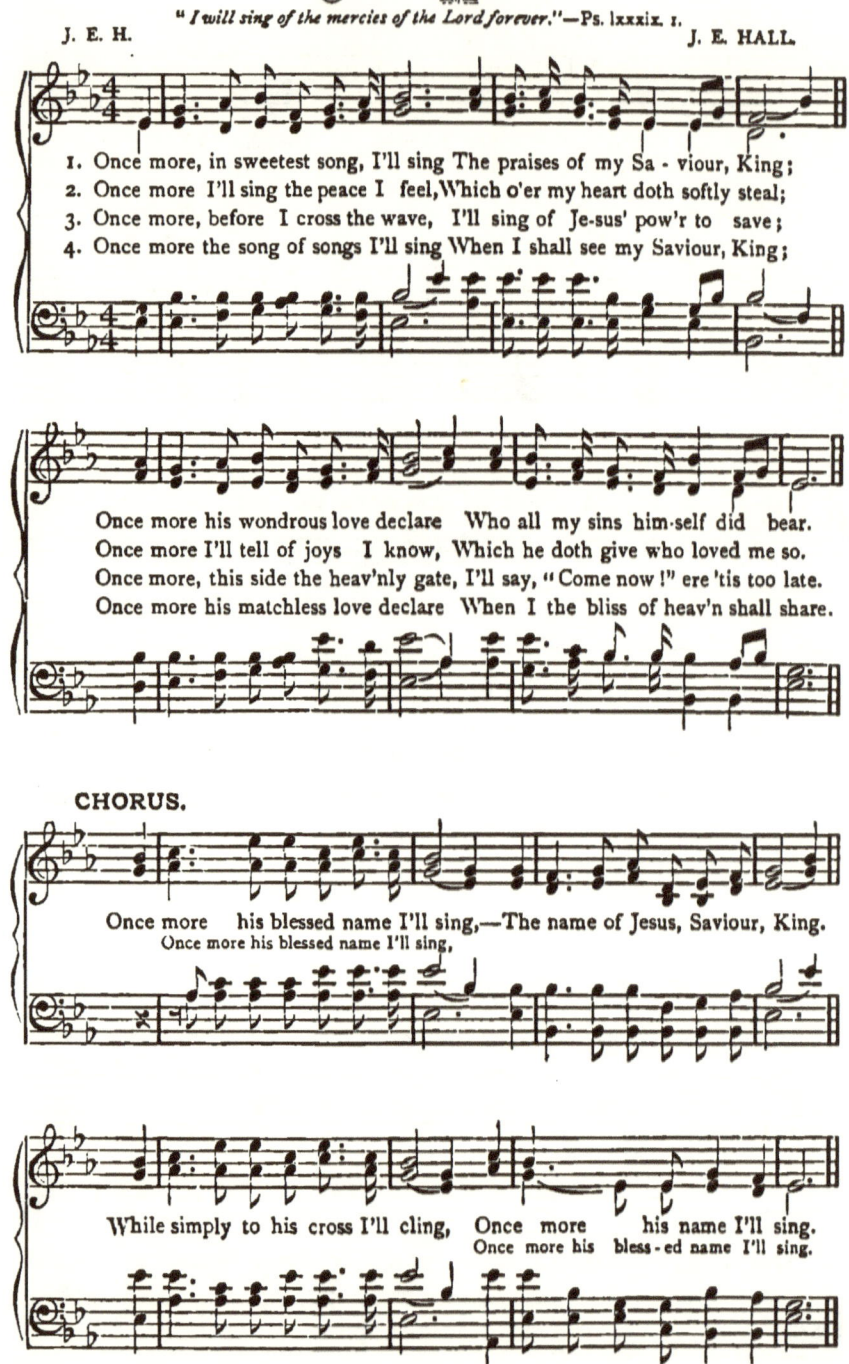

1. Once more, in sweetest song, I'll sing The praises of my Sa - viour, King;
2. Once more I'll sing the peace I feel, Which o'er my heart doth softly steal;
3. Once more, before I cross the wave, I'll sing of Je-sus' pow'r to save;
4. Once more the song of songs I'll sing When I shall see my Saviour, King;

Once more his wondrous love declare Who all my sins him-self did bear.
Once more I'll tell of joys I know, Which he doth give who loved me so.
Once more, this side the heav'nly gate, I'll say, "Come now!" ere 'tis too late.
Once more his matchless love declare When I the bliss of heav'n shall share.

CHORUS.

Once more his blessed name I'll sing,—The name of Jesus, Saviour, King.
Once more his blessed name I'll sing,

While simply to his cross I'll cling, Once more his name I'll sing.
Once more his bless-ed name I'll sing.

Reaping done.

J. E. H.   J. E. HALL.

1. When the reap - ing time is done With the set - ting of the sun,
2. With the grain all garnered in From the storms and wiles of sin,
3. Leave the sic - kles to de - cay: Fly me then to realms a - way.

And thro' Christ the vic-t'ry won, Com-eth then sweet rest and home.
We a crown of life shall win, And in heav'n find rest and home.
Where will dawn an end-less day,—Day of rest, sweet rest and home.

CHORUS.

With the reap - ing done With life's set - ting sun,
.With the reap - ing done   With life's set - ting sun,

With the vic - t'ry won Cometh rest and home.
With the vic - t'ry won,

Be not discouraged.

M. E. SERVOSS.   ADAM GEIBEL.

"I have planted, Apollos watered; but God gave the increase."—I. Cor. iii. 6.

1. Why should we be dis - cour - aged? Why let our hearts com-plain?
2. And if He to the har - vest Calls oth - ers in our stead,
3. Then leave to God the plan - ning; Per-haps if we could stand,

Why seek we for a har - vest A - mong the springing grain?
And if our ri - pened vin - tage An - oth - er comes to tread;
And see the ri - pened har - vest Throughout the Lord's broad land.

'Tis ours to do the sow - ing; 'Tis God's to give the yield;
The Fa - ther knows our tal - ents; Ap - points to each his task;
That we might claim the hon - or, The glo - ry and the fame;

Then wan-der not, com-plain - ing, A - bout the Mas - ter's field.
And strength to do His pleas - ure Is all that we should ask.
And, in our self ex - tol - ing, For - get the Fa - ther's name.

CHORUS.

So - work with ear - nest pa - tience, Each power and tal - ent wield;

Be not discouraged. CONCLUDED.

'Tis ours to do the sow - ing; 'Tis God's to give the yield.

We meet again.

F. L. ARMSTRONG.

1. We meet a - gain in glad - ness, And thank - ful voi - ces
2. We thank him for the Sab - bath,—This day of ho - ly
3. We thank him for our coun - try,— The land our Fa - thers

raise. To God, our heav'nly Fa - ther, We of - fer grate - ful
rest; And for the bless- ed Bi - ble, The book we should love
trod; For lib - er - ty of con - science And right to wor - ship

praise. 'Tis his kind hand that kept us Thro' all the chang ing
best; For Sab-bath-schools and teach - ers, To us so kind - ly
God. O Lord, our heav'nly Fa - ther, Ac - cept the praise we

year. His love it is that brings us A - gain to wor-ship here.
giv'n, To guide us in the path-way That leads to joy in heav'n.
bring; And tune our hearts and voi - ces Thy glorious name to sing.

We shall be tried.

'"When he hath tried me, I shall come forth as gold."—Job xxiii. 10.

A. S. DOUGHTY.   GEO. C. HUGG.

1. Up through tribu-la-tion   great   They the white rob'd millions came;
2. Willing to en-dure the   cross,   Will-ing more to suf-fer   shame;

They had learned to suf-fer   hate;   They had borne the Saviour's name,
Will-ing to count all things loss,   That they might the crown obtain.

They the pow'rs of earth de - fied;   They through conquest waxed bold;
Fol-low we the Cru- ci - fied   In the paths marked out of old;

In the furnace they were tried,   But from thence came forth as gold.
And when we've been fully tried,   Shall come forth as pu- rest   gold.

CHORUS.

In the furnace we'll be   tried;   From all dross be pu - ri - fied.

Je - sus will be at our side, And will bring us forth as gold.

Jesus' Little Lamb am I.

(FOR INFANT CLASS.)

ADAM GEIBEL.

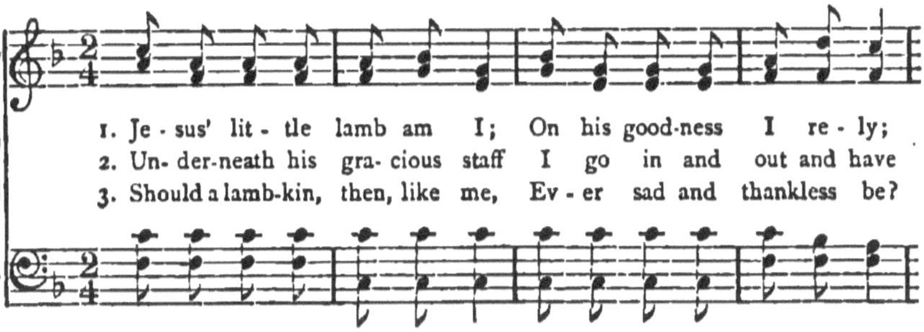

1. Je - sus' lit - tle lamb am I; On his good-ness I re - ly;
2. Un- der-neath his gra- cious staff I go in and out and have
3. Should a lamb-kin, then, like me, Ev - er sad and thankless be?

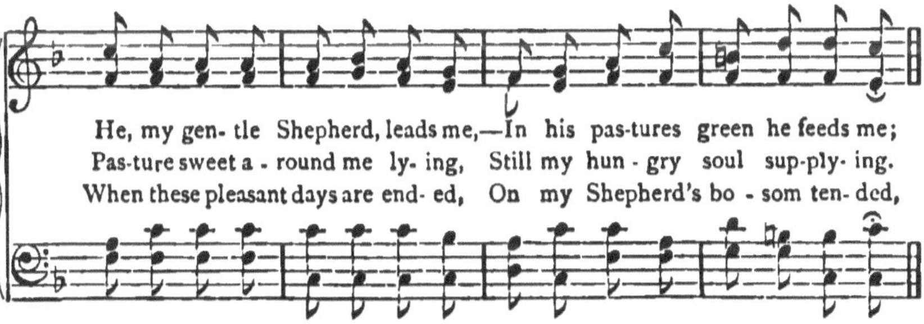

He, my gen- tle Shepherd, leads me,—In his pas-tures green he feeds me;
Pas-ture sweet a - round me ly- ing, Still my hun - gry soul sup-ply- ing.
When these pleasant days are end- ed, On my Shepherd's bo - som ten-ded,

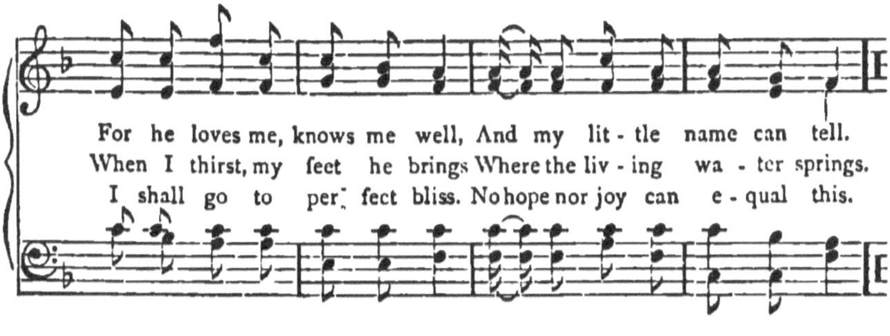

For he loves me, knows me well, And my lit - tle name can tell.
When I thirst, my feet he brings Where the liv - ing wa - ter springs.
I shall go to per- fect bliss. No hope nor joy can e - qual this.

Heaven is my Home.

ADAM GEIBEL.

1. I'm but a stran - ger here: Heav'n is my home;
2. What though the tem - pests rage: Heav'n is my home;

Earth is a des - ert drear: Heav'n is my home;
Short is my pil - grim - age: Heav'n is my home;

Dan - ger and sor - row stand Round me on ev' - ry hand,
And time's wild, win - try blast Soon will be ov - er - past,

Heav'n is my Fa - ther - land,— Heav'n is my home.
I · shall reach home at last— Heav'n is my home.

3 Therefore I murmur not:
Heaven is my home;
Whate'er my earthly lot,
Heaven is my home;
And I shall surely stand
There at my Lord's right hand:
Heaven is my Fatherland,—
Heaven is my home.

Prepare the Way.

"*Prepare ye the way of the Lord.*"—Isa. xl. 3.

J. E. H.   J. E. HALL.

Slow and boldly.

1. Pre - pare ye the way of the Lord; Make straight all the paths found therein.
2. A highway cast up for the Lord; From stones and from mire make it free.
3. Thine house set in or-der this day, That he may come in and a - bide.
4. I now hear his footsteps draw near: He comes, but so softly, to bless.

For him who in heav'n is a - dored, Wide o-pen the gates! let him in!
His com-ing must not be ig - nored; For glo-rious and kingly is he.
A Friend he will prove all life's way; In death be thy Guardian and Guide.
The King in his beanty comes here. Oh, welcome this heavenly Guest.

CHORUS.

Pre - pare for the com - ing of Je - sus, our King; With

con-cord your hearts prepare now. Make read - y to crown him Mes-

si - ah and King, Make read - y in meek-ness to bow.

Cling to the Rock.

"For they drank of that spiritual Rock that followed them, and that Rock was Christ."—Cor. x. 4.

A. S. DOUGHTY.   F. L. ARMSTRONG.

Earnestly.

1. Cling to the Rock that through a-ges long Has been the soul's Ref-uge se-cure; Cling with a faith, faith a-bid-ing and strong, That we to the end may en-dure.

2. Bathe in the Flood, the all-cleans-ing Flood,—The Foun-tain for sin o-pened wide; Drink of the stream, the life-giv-ing stream, That flows from its deep riv-en side.

3. Cling to the Rock and the prom-is-es. No mer-it nor price we can bring; The Spir-it says "come," and the call we should heed. With faith in the cross may we cling!

4. Cling to the Rock while life's dark seas roll, And waves of temp-ta-tion beat high. Cling to the safe Rest-ing place of the soul, When tri-als and dangers are nigh.

CHORUS.

Then cling to the Rock, Cling close to the Rock, Then cling to the Rock of a-ges cling. Then cling to the Rock, Cling close to the Rock, Cling to the Rock of a-ges, cling.

Hear the News.

First prize piece, from "THE INTERNATIONAL LESSON HYMNAL." By permission.

J. E. H. J. E. HALL.

Lively.

1. Hear the news, glad news of Je - sus: He is com - ing now this way.
2. Hear the news, ye blind ones, hear it. Je-sus comes your sight to given ;
3. Hear the news, oh, sad and wea - ry, He, the Lord, is now so near,
4. Hear the news, ye sick and dy - ing: Je-sus comes his power to show ;

Joy-ful tid - ings that he brings us. Hail with joy the Lord to - day.
All ye deaf and dumb, be - lieve it, And the bless-ing now re - ceive.
He will all your bur-dens car - ry, And your soul with love will cheer.
Ask his aid and trust his mer - cy : Per - fect health you then shall know.

CHORUS.

Hear the news, Hear the news, 'Tis the Saviour comes to - day,
Hear the news, Hear the news,

Hear the news, Hear the news, Now prepare without de-lay.
Hear the news, Hear the news,

Train the Children.

A. S. DOUGHTY.

GEO. C. HUGG.

"Train up a child in the way he should go."—Prov. xxii. 6.

Sprightly.

1. Train the children: guard from fall-ing: Lead them in the nar-row way.
2. Gath-er children from the highways. Snatch them from the tempter bold.
3. Train the children: love and cherish:—"He that winneth souls is wise:"

'Tis a voice from heav-en call-ing: Christian, hear it and o-bey.
Search and bring them from the by-ways,—Youthful wand'rers from the fold.
Let none wan-der, fall, or perish; Train for man-sions in the skies.

Take the child, and train it for me: Thus the Sa-viour speaks to-day;
Take and train them,—glorious du-ty. Treat them with a shepherd's care;
Train each child to be a toil-er In the Mas-ter's vineyard here;

Train it for a world of glo-ry. I, your Mas-ter, will re-pay.
Point them to the heav'n of beauty: Aid them with thy earnest prayer.
They through toil will 'scape the spoiler. Toil through grace brings triumph near.

CHORUS.

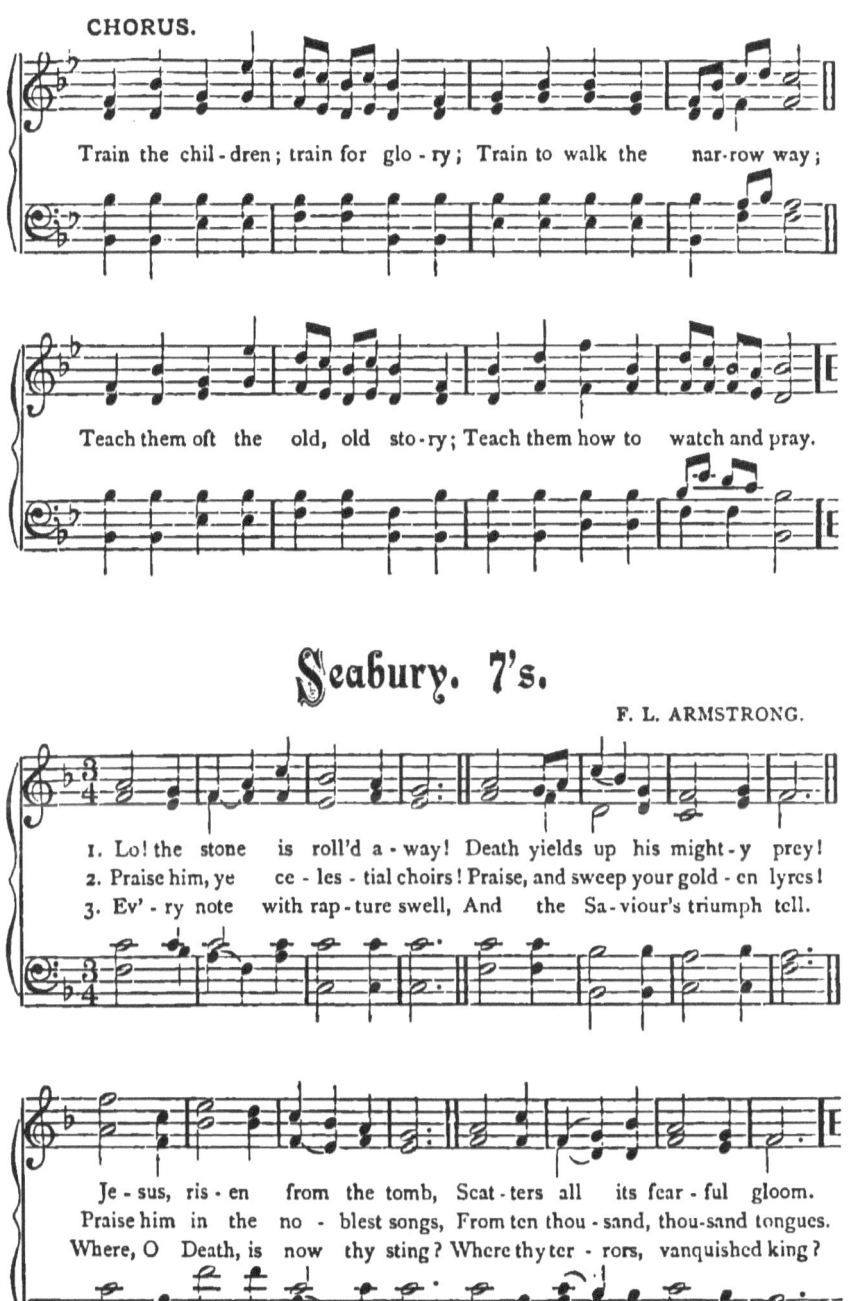

Train the chil-dren; train for glo-ry; Train to walk the nar-row way;

Teach them oft the old, old sto-ry; Teach them how to watch and pray.

Seabury. 7's.

F. L. ARMSTRONG.

1. Lo! the stone is roll'd a-way! Death yields up his might-y prey!
2. Praise him, ye ce-les-tial choirs! Praise, and sweep your gold-en lyres!
3. Ev'-ry note with rap-ture swell, And the Sa-viour's triumph tell.

Je-sus, ris-en from the tomb, Scat-ters all its fear-ful gloom.
Praise him in the no-blest songs, From ten thou-sand, thou-sand tongues.
Where, O Death, is now thy sting? Where thy ter-rors, vanquished king?

Welcome Home.

W. K. GROFF.

1. There is a realm where Jesus reigns, A home of grace and
2. There sons of earth will join to bless The pre-cious Sa-viour's
3. Yet all, a-las! may not be there, For some will slight his

love, Where an-gels wait with sweetest strains To greet the saints a-
name, Cloth'd in his per-fect righteousness, And sav'd from sin and
grace; Tho' now he calls, they do not care To turn and seek his

CHORUS.

bove.
shame. } They'll sing their welcome home to me, They'll sing their welcome
face.

home; The an-gels on the heav'n-ly strand, Will sing their welcome home.

Hark! I hear the Angels calling.

MISS MALONEY.

ADAM GEIBEL.

1. Just be-yond the roll-ing riv-er, I've a home all fair and bright; An-gels
2. Though the pathway lies through sorrow, Dan-gers all a-long the way; Oh, there
3. Of-ten sad a-long the jour-ney, Thorns oppress my wea-ry feet; Yet my

guide me safe-ly over, Where they're clothed in robes of light. There bright sunbeams gild the
is a bright to-mor-row, Perfect bliss and end-less day. For we'll meet with many
watchword shall be on-ward, For my rest-ing-place is sweet. Soon I'll drop this robe of

path-way, Beams of pure eter-nal love, And sweet flowers bloom im-mor-tal, In the
loved ones Who have crossed the path before, Sing with them the songs immor-tal, On that
sad-ness, Sing no more earth's pilgrim song. Strike a high-er note of glad-ness, Gathered

CHORUS.

pilgrim's home a-bove.
glad and hap-py shore.
with a ho-ly throng.
Hark! I hear the an-gels call-ing; Yes, they're calling me a-

way, Far a-way be-yond the riv-er, Where my kin-dred spir-its stay.

The Beautiful Gate.

ARTHUR W. FRENCH.

CHAS. D. BLAKE.

Tempo di marcia.

1. All our lov'd ones are passing a - way, Like the sweetest and fairest of
2. Oh, we cherish, in mem'ry's bright store, Happy vis - ons no time can ef-
3. In that land that is fair - est and best, Where no sorrow can ev - er be-

flow'rs, On-ly blossoming just for a day, On this sorrowful earthland of
face, Of the lost ones in glad days of yore, They who cheer'd us with beauty and
tide, We shall linger at last in sweet rest, With the lost ones again by our

Duet at lib.

ours. They are go-ing from you and from me, For no longer with us can they
grace. One by one they have faded a-way, For no longer on earth could they
side. We are wandering home one by one, To that promised land, weary and

wait ; But we know in the glad days to be, We shall meet by the beautiful gate.
wait ; But we know in some bright sunny day, We will meet by the beautiful gate.
late, And we know when our journey is done, We will meet by the beautiful gate.

CHORUS.

We will meet by the gate, by the beau - ti - ful gate, Where the

an - gels our com - ing shall wait; When we cross o'er the tide to the

sweet oth - er side, We will meet by the beau - ti - ful gate.

The Saviour died for me.

F. L. ARMSTRONG.

Andante con espressione.

1. When time seems short, and death is near, And I am press'd by doubt and fear, And
2. If grace were bought, I could not buy; If grace wers coined, no wealth have I : By
3. My faith is weak, but 'tis Thy gift; Thou canst my helpless soul up-lift. And

sins, an ev - er - last - ing tide, As-sail my peace on ev' - ry side : This
grace a-lone I draw my breath, Held up from ev - er - last - ing death. Yet
say, "Thy bonds of death are riv'n; Thy sins by Me are all for-giv'n; And

thought my ref - uge still shall be,— I know my Sa-viour died for me.
since I know His grace is free, I know the Sa-viour died for me.
thou shall live, from guilt set free; For I, thy Sa-viour, died for thee."

p CHORUS.

His name is Je - sus and he died,—For guilt-y sin - ners cru - ci-fied; Con-

ritard.

tent to die that he might win Their ransom from the death of sin.

Come, drink at the Fountain.

Present Salvation.

Rejoicing in the "fulness of God."

Words and Music by CHESTER E. POND.

1. I'll praise the Lord for joy be-low, That fills my soul to o-ver flow;
2. I'll praise the Lord for love that glows; For peace that like a riv-er flows;
3. I'll praise the Lord for His control; For love Divine that saves my soul;
4. I'll praise the Lord yet more and more While pressing toward yon Shining Shore;

I'll praise the Lord for grace Di-vine To feel and know that He is mine.
I'll praise the Lord for grace and power To live for Je-sus ev'-ry hour.
For love that guards from all my foes, For love that bears my griefs and woes.
Life's troubles sore are past and gone; I'm rest-ing now in Christ the Son.

CHORUS.

Praise ye the Lord, while a - ges roll, From sea to sea, from pole to pole.

E - ter - nal life's be - gun be - low; His joy and peace by grace I know.

I am Little.

From "THE PRIMARY S. S. TEACHER." By permission.

J. E. H.   J. F. HALL.

1. I am lit-tle, but I love, I love Je-sus, he loves me;
2. I am lit-tle, but I sing, Sing of him who came to save;
3. I am lit-tle, but I pray; Je-sus list-ens, he is nigh;
4. I am lit-tle, but I hope Up in heav'n at last to dwell;

I am lit-tle, but I love Near his precious side to be.
I am lit-tle, but I sing, Now his par-don I may have.
I am lit-tle, but I pray, And he hears my hum-ble cry.
I am lit-tle, but I hope, There for aye his praise to tell.

CHORUS.

I am lit-tle, Je-sus knows, For he sees me ev'-ry day;

I am lit-tle, Je-sus knows, So he leads me all the way.

74 More than Tongue can tell.

" Greater love hath no man than this."—JOHN xv. 13.

J. E. H.   J. E. HALL.

1. The love that Jesus had for me,— To suf-fer on the cru-el tree,
2. The ma-ny sorrows that he bore,—And oh, that crown of thorns he wore,
3. The joy I feel that he is near, The hope I have so bright and clear,
4. Oh, how I love his blessed name! In sweetest songs to sing his fame!

That I a ransomed soul might be,— Is more than tongue can tell.
That I might live for-ev-er-more,— Is more than tongue can tell.
The peace he gives without one fear, Are more than tongue can tell.
And ev'-rywhere his grace proclaim,— Yes, more than tongue can tell.

CHORUS.

His love is more than tongue can tell, His love is more than tongue can tell,
than tongue can tell,   than tongue can tell,

The love that Je-sus had for me Is more than tongue can tell.

E. F. STEWART.

ADAM GEIBEL.

1. Ho-ly Fa-ther, we a-dore thee, And all hon-or to thee give, For the bless-ings, with-out num-ber, Free-ly grant-ed while we live. In our youth-ful days thy mer-cy, Like a riv-er calmly flows, And in rip-er years ne'er fail-ing As the sol-ace of our woes.

2. Ho-ly Fa-ther, thou didst love us, E'en while wand'ring far from thee, And didst send the bless-ed Sa-viour, For a sac-ri-fice to be. In a man-ger low they laid him, 'Mid the beasts with-in the stall; An-gels guard-ing the Re-deem-er, Who sal-vation brought to all.

3. Ho-ly Fa-ther, send thy Spir-it In-to ev'-ry wait-ing heart, And let all re-ceive with fa-vor What will prove the bet-ter part. While to thee, with tune-ful voic-es, Sweetest prais-es we will sing, Heav'n and earth, in one grand cho-rus, Loudest hal-le-lu-jahs ring.

Jesus calls us.

"Go work to-day in my vineyard."—MATT. xxi. 28.

ESTRELLA.
Moderato.

GEO. C. HUGG.

1. Up and work, for Je - sus calls us, Calls to la - bor ev' -ry day;
2. Let us work and thus grow stronger, Sweetly bringing in the sheaves,—
3. When our sheaves are safely gathered From the torrent and the blast,

Let us work with earnest patience, In his ser-vice while we may.
Sheaves, if left a lit - tle lon - ger, Might be nothing more than leaves.
We shall reach the star - ry por - tal, Safe at home in heav'n at last.

CHORUS.

Up and work, for Je - sus calls us With the
Up and work, for Je - sus calls, Je - sus calls us With the

voice of love so sweet. La-bor! for each golden
voice, with the voice of love so sweet, of love so sweet; Labor! for each golden

mor - - - row Brings us near - - - er Zi-on's gate.
mor - row, gol - den mor-row, Brings us near - er, brings us near - er Zi - on's gate.

G. W. CRESSMAN.

Andante.

1. While shepherds kept their watch at night Their eyes beheld a glorious light; A
2. They next ap-pear in Herod's hall, When Herod for his wise men calls, And
3. They search the Scriptures, and they see, Thou Bethlehem shalt not least be A-
4. Then Her-od to the shepherds said, Go search and see if what was read Be

star a - rose which shone so bright It led them to see the Sa - viour.
asks, where shall this Child be born Who is to be King for - ev - er?
mong the cit - ies, for in thee Shall be born the Christ and Sa - viour.
true, that I too may be led Where the Saviour shall be wor - shiped.

CHORUS.

List to the angels! hark! how they sing, Making the heav'ns with their anthems ring,

Praising the Saviour, their great King, As they crown him Lord forev - er.

5 The Shepherds by this star were led
To where the Saviour's sacred head
Was in a stable, as was said
Should be pillowed in a manger.

6 When lo! angelic bands appear,
With heavenly voices sweet and clear!
But there should be no cause for fear,
For they sing of Christ the Saviour.

78 I have heard of a beautiful land.

J. E. H.

J. E. HALL.

SOLO.

1. I have heard of a beau-ti-ful land, With the river of life running through;
2. I have heard of a cit - y, so fair, With its streets and its walks, of pure gold,
3. I have heard of a Saviour of love, Who to save fallen man, He came down
4. Now I'm sure what I've heard, it is true, For I've found in the Bible, 'tis so,
5. Have you heard of this beautiful land? Have you heard of this city so fair?

ORGAN.

And that there on the bright, golden strand, They say, we may meet, I and you.
With its beauty there's naught can compare, And there we may dwell, I am told.
And that now, He has gone up a - bove,   To make us a home and a crown.
And this Saviour has made my heart new, Come dear friends, have your heart made new, too.
Are you wait - ing, to meet on the strand Your Saviour, your loved ones, all, there?

CHORUS.

cres.

rit.

'Tis   a beau-ti-ful land, yes, a beautiful land, And the city is grand, and so fair!

rit.

there?

And the Saviour of love, we may meet, on the strand, Shall we meet, my dear friends, over

YESUDASAN.

ADAM GEIBEL

Slowly and with emotion.

1. Whith-er, with this crushing load, Ov - er Sa-lem's dis - mal road,
2. Tell me, fainting, dy - ing Lord, Dost thou of thine own ac - cord
3. Pa-tient suf-f'rer, how can I See thee faint, and fall and die,—
4. Trembling arm and stagg'ring limb, Vis - age marr'd, eyes growing dim,

All thy bod - y suff'ring so, O my God! where dost thou go?
Bear that cross, or did thy foes, 'Gainst thy will, that load im-pose?
Gall'd and press'd and 'crush'd and ground By that cross up - on thee bound!
Tongue all parch'd, and faint at heart, Bruis'd and sore in ev' - ry part.

CHORUS.

Whith - er, Je - sus, go - est thou? Son of God, what do - est thou,

On the cit - y's "dolorous way," With that cross? O suff'rer, say.

5 Is it demon thrones to shake,
Death to kill, sin's power to break,
All our ills to put away
Life to give, and endless day?—*Chorus.*

6 Dost Thou up to Calvary go,
On that cross, in shame and woe,
Malefactors either side,
To be nailed and crucified?—*Chorus.*

He that goeth forth and weepeth.

J. E. H.

DUET.
SOP. OR ALTO.

J. E. HALL.

1. He that go - eth forth and weepeth, Bear - ing precious seed,
2. He that go - eth forth and weepeth, Trust - ing in the Lord,
3. He that go - eth forth and weepeth, All a - glow with love,
4. He that go - eth forth with weeping, Christ he nev - er leaves,

TENOR.

Let him know that as he soweth To the sinner's need, So he'll reap.
Let him know that all he soweth Of the precious word, That he'll reap.
Oft - en - times, just while he soweth, Hearts begin to move; So he'll reap.
Doubtless shall return, rejoicing! Bringing home his sheaves, Thus, he'll reap.

CHORUS.

Sow - ing now, sow - ing now, But reap - ing, by and by;

Weep - ing now, weeping now, Re - joic - ing by and by.

" There shall be no more death, neither sorrow, nor crying."—Rev. xxi. 4.

HARVEY REYNOLDS. GEO. C. HUGG.

1. Let us sing of a home o-ver there, By the side of the riv-
2. O-ver there are the friends that we love, Who before us, the val-
3. O-ver all of the vast hap-py throng, Reigns the Sa-viour in gran-
4. We shall soon reach our home o-ver there; For the end of the jour-

er of life; Where the saints of all a-ges, so fair, Are en-
ley have trod; Sweet-ly sing-ing with an-gels a-bove, Safe at
deur sub-lime; And, with faith in the prom-ise of God, Will press
ney's in view; And with friends clad in garments so fair, Through the

CHORUS.

robed in their garments of white. O-ver there, o-ver there,
home, in the pal-ace of God.
on to that heav-en-ly clime.
gates "op-en wide" will sweep through. O-ver there, o-ver there,

In the cit-y of jasper and gold, bright and fair; Where the conflicts of light

will be o'er; In that home on the gold-en shore.
o'er, will be o'er.

82 At the Gate.

J. E. H.   J. E. HALL.

1. Standing now, so near the gate, Safe with-in, I'd glad-ly be;
2. Why I wait, I can-not say, Rea-son can-not tell thee why;
3. Lov-ing friends are saying, "come," Bidding me to join their band;
4. Standing still, just by the gate, Safe with-in, I long to be;
5. At the gate, I'll wait no more, Now, just now, I'll en-ter in;

Still I stay a-way and wait, Tho' He's calling, "come to me."
Pleading Saviour, leave me, nay, Till I'm saved, no more to die.
An-gels wait, to car-ry home, The glad news to that bright land.
Shall I stay un-til too late, Till I hear "depart from me?"
Heal-ing Saviour, I im-plore, Thou wilt save me from all sin.

CHORUS.—*Earnestly.*

At the gate, near the gate, Bless-ed Sav-iour, come to me.

Cho. to 5th Thro' the gate, I will go, Bless-ed Sav-iour, comfort me.
Verse.

Waiting still, waiting still, Mighty Saviour, save, O save Thou me.

Now, just now, I'll pass thro,' Mighty Saviour! save, O save Thou me

THOMAS MACKELLAR.

ADAM GEIBEL.

1. The morn - ing stars were sing - ing With joy, when time be - gan;
2. A high - er song of glo - ry Was sung in af - ter - time,—
3. A mul - ti-tude of voic - es Have learn'd this ho - ly song;

And heav'n - ly peals were ring - ing, When God crea - a - ted man
And shep- herds heard the sto - ry, Re- hears'd in sounds sub - lime,—
And earth with heav'n re - joic - es, To roll the sound a - long.

The u - ni-verse was swell - ing, With ju - bi-lant de - light,
Of Je - sus in a man - ger, God's well - be-lov - ed Son,
With saints and an - gels o'er us, Who sing by us un - heard,

While all to all were tell - ing Je - ho - vah's pow'r and might.
Who came to save from dan - ger A race by sin un - done.
We join the glad-some cho - rus, And ech - o ev' - ry word.

Work!

"Go work to-day in my vineyard."—MATT. xxi, 28.

ANON.   F. L. ARMSTRONG.

Go work in my vine-yard! there's plen ty to do. The
Go work in my vine-yard! I claim thee as mine. With
Go work in my vine-yard! oh, work while 'tis day! The

har - vest is great and the la - b'rers are few. There's
blood did I buy thee and all that is thine. Thy
bright hours of sun - shine are hast'ning a - way; And

weed - ing and fenc - ing and clear - ing of roots, And
time and thy tal - ents, thy lof - tiest powers,— Thy
night's gloom - y shad - ows are gath - er - ing fast; Then the

ploughing and sow - ing, and gath'r-ing of fruits. There are
warmest af - fec - tions, thy sun - ni - est hours. I
time for our la - bor shall ev - er be past. Be -

fox - es to take; There are wolves to de - stroy. All
will - ing - ly yield - ed my kingdom for thee; The
gin in the morn - ing and toil all the day. Thy

·a - ges and ranks I can ful - ly em - ploy. I've
song of arch - an - gels to hang on the tree. In
strength I'll sup - ply and thy wa - ges I'll pay. And

sheep to be tended and lambs to be fed : The lost must be gather'd ; The
pain and tempta-tion, in anguish and shame, I paid thee full ransom. My
blessed, thrice blessed the di - li - gent few Who fin - ish the labor I've

CHORUS.

weary ones led.
purchase I claim. } Go work in my vine - yard! Go
giv'n them to do.

Go work in my vine-yard! there's plen-ty to do. The

work in my vine - yard! The har - vest is
harvest is great and the la - b'rers are few. Go work in my vine-yard! there's

great and the la - b'rers are few.
plen-ty to do. The har - vest is great and the la - b'rers are few.

The Morning Light.

EDGAR PAGE. JNO. R. SWENEY.

Tempo di marcia.

1. See the morning light is break - ing O'er the east - ern sky.
2. Hal - le - lu - jah! vic - t'ry dawn - eth. Lis - ten to the word.
3. Ar - my of the Lord a - noin - ted, Get the ar - mor on;

See the clouds of sin are scat - ter'd; And be - fore it fly.
Hark! we hear the ar - my shout - ing, Glo - ry to the Lord!
Read - y moun - ted for the con - flict, When the light shall dawn,

Oh, thou Sun of full sal - va - tion, Pour thy gold - en ray
Christ, our Cap - tain, or - ders "For - ward!" On, ye chos - en band!
All a - bout the hosts are arm - ing, And the bless - ed word,

O'er this wait - ing, watching na - tion. Let it come to - day!
With our lead - er ful - ly a - ble, To pos - sess the land.
All a - long the ranks is pass - ing, Glo - ry to the Lord.

CHORUS.

Swell the cho - rus, glad and glo - rious,
Yes, swell the cho - rus, Yes, glad and glo - rious,

O'er the earth and o'er the sea; Full sal - va - tion,

ev' - [ry na - tion Ho - ly to the Lord shall be.

4 Lift aloft the blood-stained banner,
Banner of the cross;
None that march beneath this ensign
Ever suffer loss,
Forward, every Christian soldier,
Consecrated host,
Trusting in our God the Father,
Son, and Holy Ghost.

Hauser. L. M.

CHESTER E. POND.

F. L. ARMSTRONG.

1. My mind is stayed on God a-lone; In perfect peace he keeps his own;
2. His conscious love, so deep and full, Pervades entire my in-most soul;
3. What perfect love, by grace, I know; It casts out fear while here be-low;

His ho-ly Word now glows with light: I walk by faith, and not by sight.
The more I crave this boundless love, The more he gives me from a-bove.
It fills my soul with rapturous song Before I reach yon heavenly throng.

88 Gather with Glad Hearts and Voices.

P. P. A.

F. L. ARMSTRONG.

Maestoso.

1. Gath- er with glad hearts and voic-es, Free-ly come from far and 'near;
2. Come and bring your choicest off 'rings; Lay them humbly at his feet;
3. Let our hearts with love o'erflow-ing For the kindness to us shown

Na- ture now it - self re - joic-es, And bright heav'nly hosts ap- pear.
But pre-sent no ran - dom gath'rings, For the best are hard-ly meet.
By our God, the great Cre - a - tor, Prais-es sing to him a - lone.

Hear the gladsome song of triumph, Christ, our King, is born to-day!
Flow-ers bright and gar-lands handsome, Mosses fresh and i - vy green:
Prais - es, then, to Christ, our Sa - viour, On this hap-py Christmas day.

Shout a-loud the glo - rious tid-ings! Let us drive all fear a - way.
They will make our tem - ple winsome, And enhance the cheerful scene.
May we strive to do his pleasure! Let us try, as best we may.

I know no Life divided.

89

MASSEY.

"I will praise the Lord with my whole heart."—Ps. iii. 1.

W. A. OGDEN.

1. I know no life di - vi - ded, O Lord of life, from thee; In thee is life pro - vi - ded For all mankind and me. I know no death, O Je - sus, Be - cause I live in thee: Thy death it is which frees us From death e - ter - nal - ly.

2. I fear no trib - u - la - tion Since, what - so - e'er it be, It makes no sep - a - ra - tion Be - tween my Lord and me. If thou, my God and Teach - er, Vouch-safe to be my own, 'Though poor, I should be rich - er Than mon - arch on his throne.

3. Lord, with this truth im - press me, And write it on my heart, To com - fort, cheer and bless me, That thou my Sa - viour art. With - out thy love to guide me, I should be whol - ly lost: The floods would quickly hide me, On life's wide o - cean tossed.

The Lord may come to-day.

J. B.

J. BAKER.

1. Bus-y ser-vant in the vineyard, Earnest sol-dier in the fray,
2. Are you bus-y, all too bus-y With the things that fade a-way—

Cheer your heart, and, up-ward glancing, Think—the Lord may come to-day.
Wealth, or fame, or gain, or pleas-ure? Drop them, He may come to-day.

Weak and wea-ry troubled mourner, Fear-ing dan-gers in the way,
Or an i-dler in the vineyard,—Oth-ers pass you on the way?

Be no long-er sin-ful car-ing, For the Lord may come to-day.
Wake, and live as an im-mor-tal, Lest the Lord should come to-day.

CHORUS.

Are we waiting, are we waiting, Yes, we're
Yes, we're waiting, Yes, we're waiting,

waiting for the hap-py, hap-py time, When the bless-ed Lord shall come a-

gain in the clouds To gath-er all his chil-dren home.

3 Is the blood upon your garments;
Have you on His pure array?
Naught can hide a guilty sinner,
If in light He come to-day.
Are you waiting for the Master?
He is surely on His way;
We can almost hear His footfall.
Blessed Jesus! come to-day.

Howe. 8s & 7s.

F. L. ARMSTRONG.

Andante.

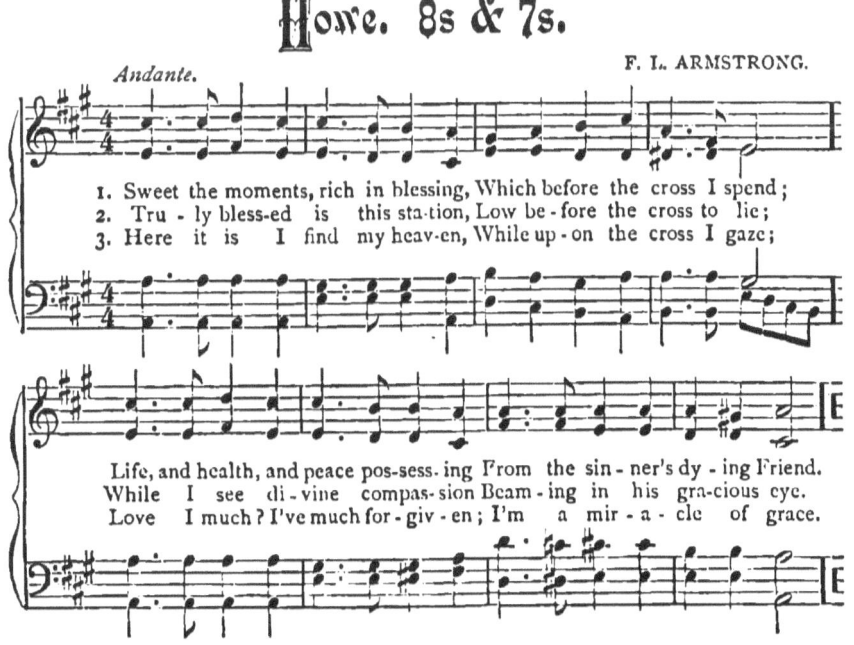

1. Sweet the moments, rich in blessing, Which before the cross I spend;
2. Tru-ly bless-ed is this sta-tion, Low be-fore the cross to lie;
3. Here it is I find my heav-en, While up-on the cross I gaze;

Life, and health, and peace pos-sess-ing From the sin-ner's dy-ing Friend.
While I see di-vine compas-sion Beam-ing in his gra-cious eye.
Love I much? I've much for-giv-en; I'm a mir-a-cle of grace.

Song of the Saints.

"There is a friend that sticketh closer than a brother."—Prov. xviii. 24.

GEO. C. HUGG.

Con espressione.

1. There's a Friend a - bove all oth - ers. Oh, how he loves!
2. Bless - ed Je - sus! wouldst thou know him? Oh, how he loves!
3. Pause, my soul! a - dore and won - der. Oh, how he loves!
4. Let us still this love be view - ing. Oh, how he loves!

His is love be - yond a broth - er's. Oh, how he loves!
Give thy - self e'en this day to him. Oh, how he loves!
Naught can cleave this love a - sun - der. Oh, how he loves!
And, though faint, keep on pur - su - ing. Oh, how he loves!

Earth-ly friends may fail and leave us: This day kind, the next bereave us;
Is it sin that pains and grieves thee? Doubts and tri-als, do they tease thee?
Neither tri - als, nor tempta - tion, Doubt, nor fear, nor trib - u - la - tion,
He will strengthen each endeav - or, And when pass'd o'er Jordan's riv-er,

But this Friend will ne'er de - ceive us. Oh, how he loves!
Je - sus can from all re - lease thee. Oh, how he loves!
Can de - prive us of sal - va - tion. Oh, how he loves!
This shall be our song for - ev - er. Oh, how he loves!

Poor and needy.

93

" I am poor and needy."—Ps. lxxxvi. 1.

J. E. H.

J. E. HALL.

1. Bow thine ear, O Lord, and hear me! Un-to thee I lift my soul.
2. Bow thine ear down in thy mer-cy; For to thee I daily cry.

I am poor and I am needy, Sick, and dying, make me whole.
To my heart, so full of shadow, Do not now thy smile de-ny.

CHORUS.

I am poor and I am needy. Thou art rich, to thee I cry.

I am poor and I am needy. Help me, Saviour, ere I die.

3 Thou art full of mercy, blessings,
Free to all who will receive;
Let these blessings fall upon me;
Peace and pardon, Jesus, give.

4 I will praise thee for thy goodness,—
For thy love so great to me;
Thou didst see me bound in fetters;
Didst unbind and make me free.

Papa, come.*

J. E. H.

J. E. HALL.

Slow.

1. 'Tis but just a - cross the riv - er, In that an - gel land so fair,
2. Still an - oth - er lamb He's tak - en, In His tend - er lov - ing arms,
3. I can see now why He took them to that blessed heav'n - ly home;

Where the Saviour ev - er liv - eth, Who on earth our sins didst bear.
And she beckons now un - to me With her most en - tic - ing charms.
'Twas to make me know the Sav - iour And to heed his loving, "Come!"

Where the saved ones gone be - fore us, In white gar - ments do ap - pear;
For I'm sure, she's safe with Je - sus, Safe from fear and all a - larms;
So that when I cross the riv - er, I shall al - ways be at home

CHORUS.

There's our Wil - lie, he's up there, And I hear him call - ing:
There's our Nel - lie, she's up there, And I hear her call - ing:
With the loved ones o - ver there, Still I hear them call - ing:

"Pa - pa, come! Oh, 'tis beau - ti - ful, 'tis beau - ti - ful up here."

* A gentleman, having had two children taken away, felt that they were calling him.

"Come this way, dear papa, come, please come. Come, dear papa, to this land so fair."

Go in peace.

" Thy faith hath saved thee ; go in peace."—LUKE vii. 50.

J. E. H.   J. E. HALL.

DUET. Soprano and Alt.

1. "Go in peace, thy faith hath saved thee," Hear the blessed Sa - viour say
2. And her eyes, bedimmed with weeping, Now with joy be - gin to light,

To that weep - ing, out - cast woman: Then with joy she went her way.
As the sun - shine af - ter sha - dow; As the dawn-ing af - ter night.

CHORUS.

Go in peace! go in peace! Hear the bless - ed Sa - viour say;

Go in peace! go in peace! With re - joic - ing, go thy way!

3 Oh, what peace now follows warfare,
   For the blessed Christ has blest:
Joy succeeds the bitter mourning ;
   Love unmeasured fills her breast.

4 Wouldst thou, wanderer, know this Saviour?
   "Go in peace!" wouldst hear him say ?
Come in faith and with contrition :
   Then, rejoicing, go thy way.

Jesus, Lover of my Soul.

ADAM GEIBEL.

Andante quasilento.

Je - sus, Lov - er of my soul,

Let me to thy bo - som fly, While the near - er

wa - ters roll, While the tem - pest still is high.

Soprano Solo.

Hide me, O my Sa - viour, hide, Till the storm of life is past;

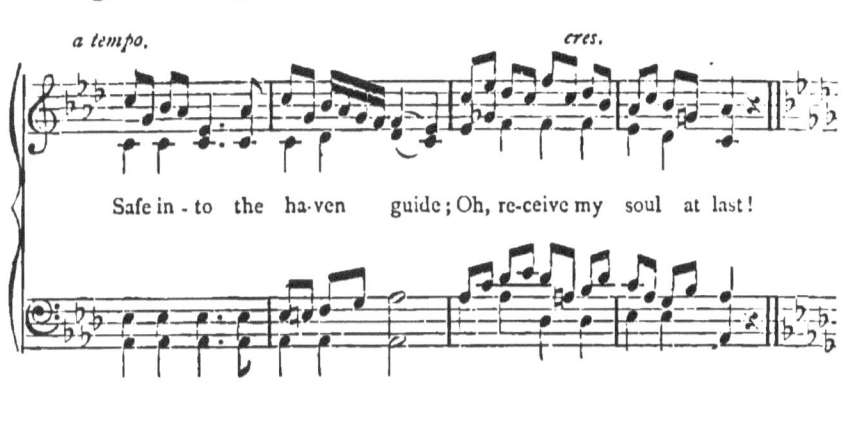

Safe in - to the ha-ven guide; Oh, re-ceive my soul at last!

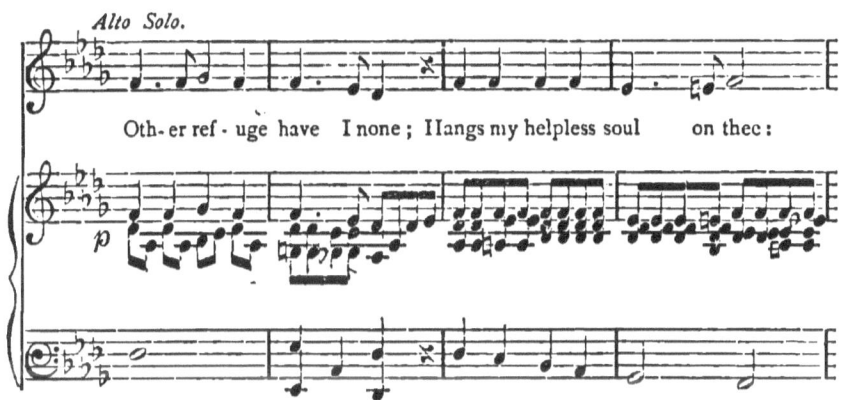

Oth- er ref - uge have I none ; Hangs my helpless soul on thee :

Leave, ah, leave me not a - lone. Still support and comfort me !

Jesus, Lover of my Soul. CONCLUDED.

All my trust on thee is stay'd: All my help from

thee I bring. Cov - er my de - fence - less head

With the shad - ow of thy wing. Je - sus,

Je - sus, Lov - er,

Lov-er of my soul, Let me to thy bo - som fly.

of my soul,

Arlington. C. M.

Rev. ISAAC WATTS. THOS. A. ARNE.

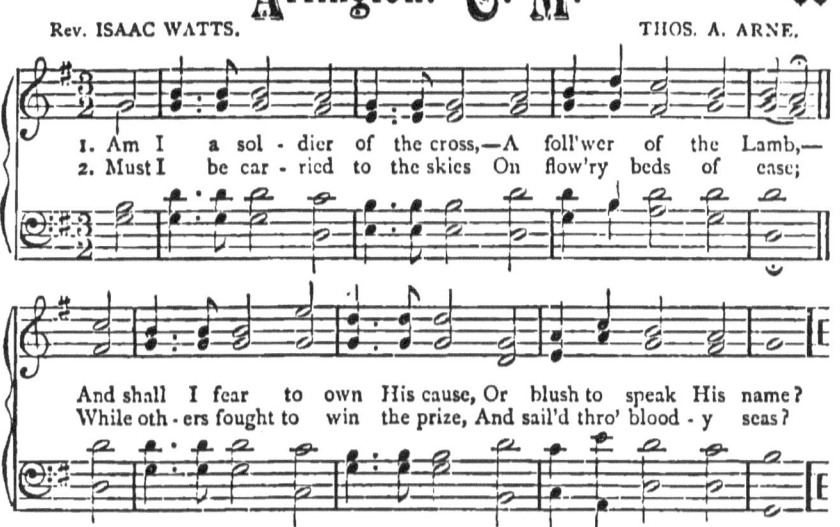

1. Am I a sol - dier of the cross,—A foll'wer of the Lamb,—
2. Must I be car - ried to the skies On flow'ry beds of ease;

And shall I fear to own His cause, Or blush to speak His name?
While oth - ers fought to win the prize, And sail'd thro' blood - y seas?

3 Are there no foes for me to face?
  Must I not stem the flood?
Is this vile world a friend to grace,
  To help me on to God?

4 Since I must fight if I would reign,
  Increase my courage, Lord;
I'll bear the toil, endure the pain,
  Supported by Thy word.

Dundee. C. M.

Rev. ISAAC WATTS. GUILLAUME FRANC.

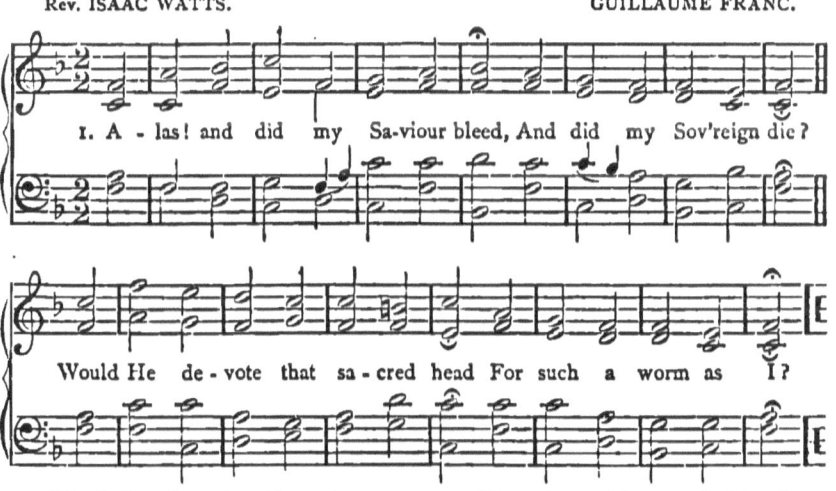

1. A - las! and did my Sa - viour bleed, And did my Sov'reign die?

Would He de - vote that sa - cred head For such a worm as I?

2 Was it for crimes that I have done,
  He groan'd upon the tree?
Amazing pity! grace unknown!
  And love beyond degree!

3 Well might the sun in darkness hide,
  And shut his glories in,
When Christ, the mighty Maker died,
  For man, the creature's sin.

4 Thus might I hide my blushing face
  While His dear cross appears;
Dissolve my heart in thankfulness,
  And melt mine eyes to tears.

5 But drops of grief can ne'er repay
  The debt of love I owe:
Here, Lord, I give myself away,—
  'Tis all that I can do.

Old Hundred. L. M.

LUTHER.

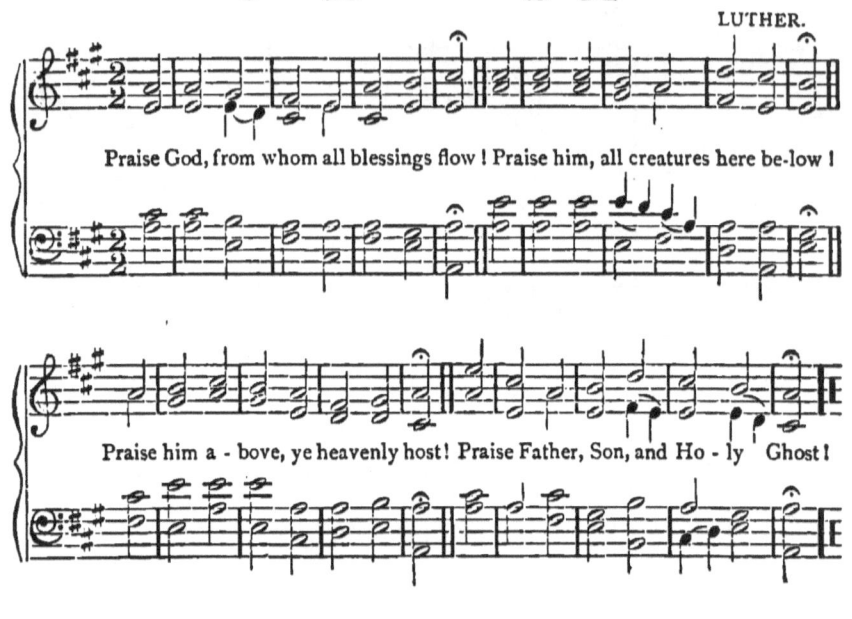

Praise God, from whom all blessings flow ! Praise him, all creatures here be-low !

Praise him a - bove, ye heavenly host ! Praise Father, Son, and Ho - ly Ghost !

Duke Street. L. M.

HATTON.

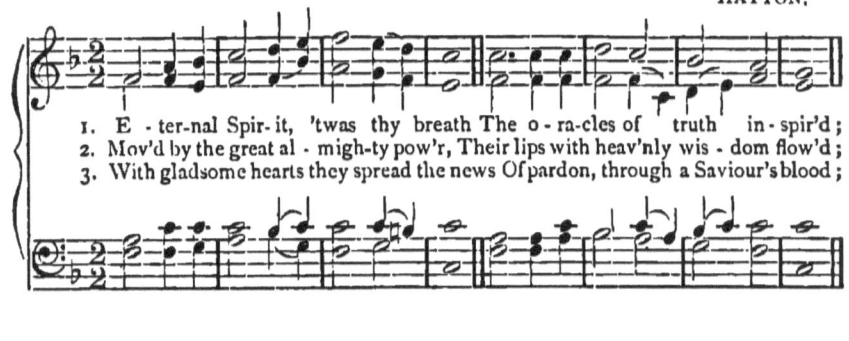

1. E - ter-nal Spir- it, 'twas thy breath The o - ra-cles of   truth   in - spir'd ;
2. Mov'd by the great al - migh-ty pow'r, Their lips with heav'nly wis - dom flow'd ;
3. With gladsome hearts they spread the news Of pardon, through a Saviour's blood ;

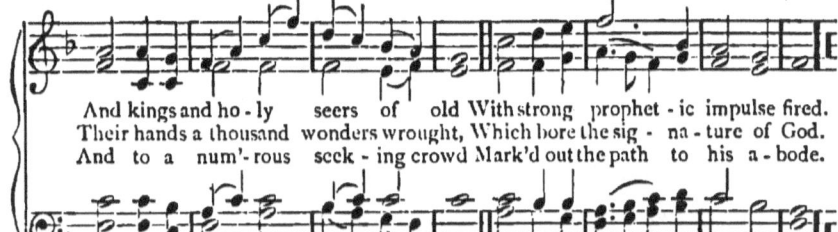

And kings and ho - ly   seers of   old With strong prophet - ic impulse fired.
Their hands a thousand wonders wrought, Which bore the sig - na - ture of God.
And to a num'- rous   seek - ing crowd Mark'd out the path to his a - bode.

S. F. SMITH. HANDEL.

1. My country, 'tis of thee, Sweet land of lib-er-ty, Of thee I sing: Land where my
2. My na-tive coun-try, thee—Land of the noble free—Thy name I love: I love thy
3. Our fathers' God! to thee, Author of lib-er-ty, To thee we sing: Long may our

fathers died, Land of the pilgrim's pride, From every mountain side Let freedom ring!
rocks and rills, Thy woods and templed hills; My heart with rapture thrills Like that above.
land be bright With freedom's holy light; Protect us by thy might, Great God, our King!

Italian Hymn. 6s & 4s.

MADAN. GIARDINI.

1. Come, thou al-might-y King, Help us Thy name to sing, Help us to praise!
2. Come, ho-ly Com-fort-er, Thy sa-cred wit-ness bear, In this glad hour;
3. To Thee, great One in Three, The highest prais-es be, Hence ev-er-more;

Father all glo-ri-ous, O'er all victorious, Come and reign over us, Ancient of days.
Thou, who almighty art, Now rule in every heart, And ne'er from us depart, Spirit of pow'r.
Thy sovereign majesty May we in glory see, And to e-ter-ni-ty Love and adore.

Rockingham. L. M.

WM. COWPER.   LOWELL MASON.

1. What various hin-dran-ces we meet In coming to the mer-cy seat!

Yet who that knows the worth of prayer, But wishes to be of-ten there?

2 Prayer makes the darkened clouds withdraw;
Prayer climbs the ladder Jacob saw;
Gives exercise to faith and love;
Brings every blessing from above.

3 Restraining prayer, we cease to fight;
Prayer makes the Christian's armor bright;
And Satan trembles when he sees
The weakest saint upon his knees.

Mendon. L. M.

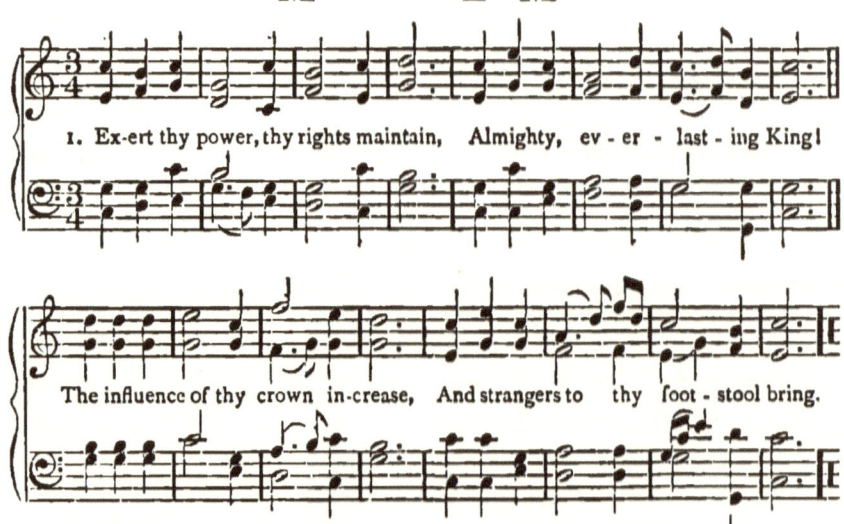

1. Ex-ert thy power, thy rights maintain, Almighty, ev-er-last-ing King!

The influence of thy crown in-crease, And strangers to thy foot-stool bring.

2 In one vast symphony of praise,
Gentile and Jew shall then unite,
And unbelief no longer reign,
But sink in shades of endless night.

3 Then Afric's liberated sons,
Shall chant to Asia's rapturous song,
Europe resound her Saviour's fame,
And western climes the notes prolong.

Laban. S. M.

GEO. HEATH.   LOWELL MASON.

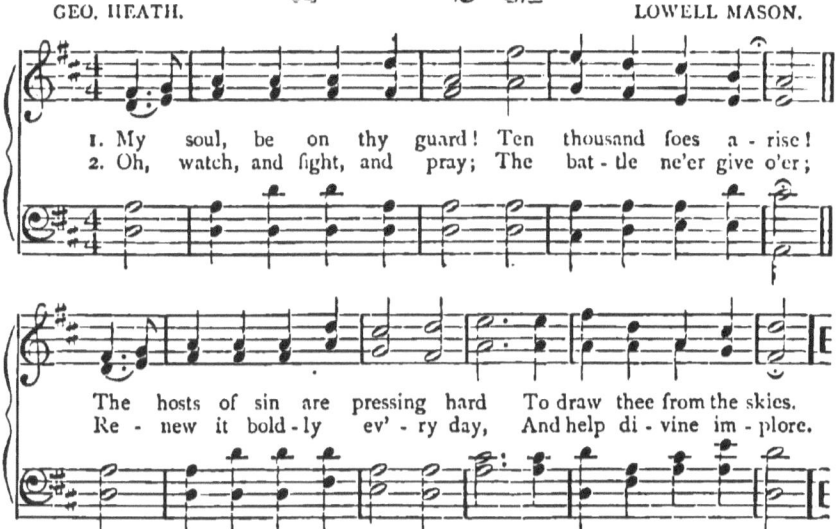

1. My soul, be on thy guard! Ten thousand foes a - rise!
2. Oh, watch, and fight, and pray; The bat - tle ne'er give o'er;

The hosts of sin are pressing hard   To draw thee from the skies.
Re - new it bold - ly ev' - ry day,   And help di - vine im - plore.

3 Ne'er think the vict'ry won,
  Nor lay thine armor down;
  Thine arduous work will not be done
  Till thou obtain thy crown.

4 Then persevere till death
  Shall bring thee to thy God;
  He'll take thee, at thy parting breath,
  To His divine abode.

Dennis. S. M.

Rev. JOHN FAWCETT.   H. G. NAGELI.

1. Blest be the tie that binds   Our hearts in Chris - tian love;
2. Be - fore our Fa - ther's throne, We pour our ar - dent prayers;

The fel - low - ship of kin - dred minds   Is like to that a - bove.
Our fears, our hopes, our aims are one,—   Our com - forts and our cares.

3 We share our mutual woes;
  Our mutual burdens bear;
  And often for each other flows
  The sympathizing tear.

4 When we asunder part,
  It gives us inward pain ;
  But we shall still be join'd in heart,
  And hope to meet again.

Amsterdam. 7s & 6s.

1. Rise, my soul, and stretch thy wings, Thy bet-ter por-tion trace;
2. Ri-vers to the o-cean run, Nor stay in all their course:
3. Cease, ye pil-grims, cease to mourn. Press on-ward to the prize.

Rise from tran-si-to-ry things Toward heav'n, thy na-tive place:
Fire as-cend-ing seeks the sun; Both speed them to their source:
Soon your Sa-viour will re-turn, Tri-umph-ant in the skies:

Sun and moon and stars de-cay: Time shall soon this earth re-move:
So a soul that's born of God Pants to view his glo-rious face,
Yet a sea-son, and you know Hap-py en-trance will be giv'n;

Rise, my soul, and haste a-way To seats pre-pared a-bove.
Up-wards tends to his a-bode To rest in his em-brace.
All your sor-rows left be-low, And earth exchanged for heav'n.

WATTS.   HAYDN.

1. From all that dwell be-low the skies, Let the Cre -
2. Your lof-ty themes, ye mor-tals, bring: In songs of
3. In ev'-ry land be-gin the song: To ev'-ry
4. E - ter-nal are thy mer-cies, Lord: E - ter-nal

a - tor's praise a - rise! Let the Re-deemer's name be sung
praise di - vine-ly sing. The great sal - va - tion loud proclaim,
land the strains be - long. In cheer-ful sounds all voic - es raise
truth at - tends thy word. Thy praise shall sound from shore to shore

Through ev' - ry land by ev' - ry tongue! Let the Re-
And shout for joy the Sa - viour's name. The great sal-
And fill the world with loud - est praise. In cheer - ful
Till suns shall rise and set no more. Thy praise shall

deem - er's name be sung Through ev' - ry land by ev' - ry tongue.
va - tion loud proclaim, And shout for joy the Saviour's name.
sounds all voic - es raise And fill the world with loudest praise.
sound from shore to shore Till suns shall rise and set no more.

I Know.

" I shall be satisfied, when I awake, with thy likeness."—Ps. xvii. 15.

J. E. H.   J. E. HALL.

Solo.

1. Oh, I know that I sometime shall see him, My Re-
2. Oh, I know there'll be joy and for - ev - er In that
3. Oh, I know that with an - gels in glo - ry I shall
4. Oh, I know I shall nev - er be wea - ry, If on

rit.

deemer and Sa - viour and Lord; In that par - a - dise land I shall
won-der - ful heav'n-land of song; When the dear ones shall meet ne'er to
al-ways be hap - py and blest; Then thro' a - ges I'll sing sweet the
Je - sus I once fix mine eye; And the days there will never be

rit.

greet him, Whom so long I have lov'd and a - dor'd.
sev - er, And in prais-es join with that vast throng.
sto - ry, While from tri - als and care I shall rest.
drea - ry, For in bliss I shall reign, aye and aye.

rit.

Oh, I know that just o - ver the riv - er, There my Saviour's dear face, I shall see. Oh, I know that just o - ver the riv - er There for - ev - er with him I shall be.

1 Rock of Ages, cleft for me,
  Let me hide myself in thee;
  Let the water and the blood,
  From thy riven side which flowed,
  Be of sin the double cure,
  Save me from its guilt and power.

2 Not the labor of my hands
  Can fulfil the law's demands;
  Could my zeal no respite know,
  Could my tears forever flow,
  All for sin could not atone:
  Thou must save, and thou alone.

3 Nothing in my hand I bring,
  Simply to thy cross I cling;
  Naked, come to thee for dress,
  Helpless, look to thee for grace;
  Foul, I to the fountain fly:
  Wash me, Saviour, or I die.

4 While I draw this fleeting breath,
  When mine eyes shall close in death,
  When I soar to worlds unknown,
  See thee on thy judgment throne—
  Rock of Ages, cleft for me,
  Let me hide myself in thee.

1 Sweet hour of prayer! sweet hour of prayer!
  That calls me from a world of care,
  And bids me at my Father's throne
  Make all my wants and wishes known;
  In seasons of distress and grief,
  My soul has often found relief,
  |: And oft escaped the tempter's snare,
  By thy return, sweet hour of prayer.:|

2 Sweet hour of prayer! sweet hour of prayer!
  Thy wings shall my petition bear
  To him whose truth and faithfulness
  Engage the waiting soul to bless.
  And since he bids me seek his face,
  Believe his word, and trust his grace,
  |: I'll cast on him my every care,
  And wait for thee, sweet hour of prayer!:|

3 Sweet hour of prayer! sweet hour of prayer!
  May I thy consolation share,
  Till, from Mount Pisgah's lofty height,
  I view my home and take my flight;
  This robe of flesh I'll drop, and rise
  To seize the everlasting prize;
  |: And shout, while passing through the air,
  Farewell, farewell, sweet hour of prayer!:|

1 Jesus, Lover of my soul,
   Let me to thy bosom fly,
 While the nearer waters roll,
   While the tempest still is high ;
 Hide me, O my Saviour, hide,
   Till the storm of life is past ;
 Safe into the haven guide,
   Oh, receive my soul at last.

2 Other refuge have I none,
   Hangs my helpless soul on thee :
 Leave, oh, leave me not alone,
   Still support and comfort me.
 All my trust on thee is stayed,
   All my help from thee I bring,
 Cover my defenceless head
   With the shadow of thy wing.

3 Thou, O Christ, art all I want ;
   More than all in thee I find :
 Raise the fallen, cheer the faint,
   Heal the sick, and lead the blind.
 Just and Holy is thy name,
   I am all unrighteousness :
 Vile, and full of sin I am,
   Thou art full of truth and grace.

4 Plenteous grace with thee is found,—
   Grace to cover all my sin :
 Let the healing streams abound ;
   Make and keep me, pure within.
 Thou of life the Fountain art,
   Freely let me take of thee :
 Spring thou up within my heart ;
   Rise to all eternity.

1 Come, Holy Spirit, heavenly Dove !
   With all thy quickening powers ;
 Kindle a flame of heavenly love
   In these cold hearts of ours.

2 Dear Lord ! and shall we ever live
   At this poor dying rate ?
 Our love so faint, so cold to thee,
   And thine to us so great ?

3 Come, Holy Spirit, heavenly Dove,
   With all thy quickening powers ;
 Come, shed abroad a Saviour's love,
   And that shall kindle ours.

1 Come, thou Fount of every blessing,
   Tune my heart to sing thy grace ;
 Streams of mercy, never ceasing,
   Call for songs of loudest praise ;
 Teach me some melodious sonnet,
   Sung by flaming tongues above ;
 Praise the mount—I'm fixed upon it !
   Mount of thy redeeming love.

2 Here I'll raise my Ebenezer,
   Hither by thy help I'm come :
 And I hope, by thy good pleasure,
   Safely to arrive at home.
 Jesus sought me when a stranger,
   Wandering from the fold of God :
 He to rescue me from danger,
   Interposed his precious blood.

3 Oh, to grace how great a debtor,
   Daily I'm constrained to be !
 Let thy goodness, as a fetter,
   Bind my wandering heart to thee.
 Prone to wander, Lord, I feel it,—
   Prone to leave the God I love,—
 Here's my heart, oh, take and seal it,
   Seal it for thy courts above.

1 Just as I am, without one plea,
   But that thy blood was shed for me,
 And that thou bidd'st me come to thee,
   O Lamb of God ! I come, I come !

2 Just as I am, and waiting not
   To rid my soul of one dark blot,
 To thee, whose blood can cleanse each spot,
   O Lamb of God ! I come, I come !

3 Just as I am, though tossed about,
   With many a conflict, many a doubt,
 Fightings and fears within, without,
   O Lamb of God ! I come, I come !

4 Just as I am, poor, wretched, blind,
   Sight, riches, healing of the mind,
 Yea, all I need, in thee to find,
   O Lamb of God ! I come, I come !

5 Just as I am, thou wilt receive,
   Wilt welcome, pardon, cleanse, relieve ;
 Because thy promise I believe,
   O Lamb of God ! I come, I come !

1 Come, said Jesus' sacred voice,
Come, and make my paths your choice;
I will guide you to your home;
Weary pilgrim, hither come.

2 Thou who, houseless, sole, forlorn,
Long hast borne the proud world's scorn,
Long hast roam'd the barren waste :
Weary pilgrim, hither haste.

3 Ye, by fiercer anguish torn,
Guilt, in strong remorse, who mourn,
Here repose your heavy care :
Conscience wounded who can bear ?

4 Sinners, come, for here is found
Balm that flows for ev'ry wound ;
Peace that ever shall endure ;
Rest eternal, sacred, sure.

———

1 Nearer, my God, to thee,
Nearer to thee !
E'en though it be a cross
That raiseth me ;
Still all my song shall be,—
Nearer, my God, to thee !
Nearer to thee !

2 Though, like the wanderer,
The sun gone down,
Darkness be over me,
My rest a stone ;
Yet in my dreams I'd be
Nearer, my God, to thee !
Nearer to thee !

3 There let the way appear,
Steps unto heaven ;
All that thou sendest me,
In mercy given ;
Angels to beckon me
Nearer, my God, to thee !
Nearer to thee !

4 Then with my waking thoughts,
Bright with thy praise,
Out of my stony griefs,
Bethel I'll raise ;
So by my woes to be
Nearer, my God, to thee !
Nearer to thee !

5 Or if on joyful wing,
Cleaving the sky,
Sun moon, and stars forgot,
Upward I fly ;
Still all my song shall be,—
Nearer, my God, to thee !
Nearer to thee !

1 O happy day that fixed my choice
On thee, my Saviour and my God !
Well may this glowing heart rejoice,
And tell its raptures all abroad.

CHORUS.—Happy day, happy day,
When Jesus washed my sins away ;
He taught me how to watch and pray,
And live rejoicing every day,
Happy day, happy day,
When Jesus washed my sins away.

2 'Tis done, the great transaction's done—
I am my Lord's, and he is mine ;
He drew me, and I followed on,
Charmed to confess the voice divine. *Cho.*

3 Now rest, my long-divided heart ;
Fixed on this blissful centre, rest ;
Nor ever from thy Lord depart,
With him of every good possessed. *Cho.*

4 High heaven, that heard the solemn vow,
That vow renewed shall daily hear,
Till in life's latest hour I bow,
And bless in death a bond so dear. *Cho.*

———

1 Work, for the night is coming ;
Work through the morning hours ;
Work, while the dew is sparkling ;
Work, 'mid springing flowers ;
Work, when the day grows brighter ;
Work, in the glowing sun ;
Work, for the night is coming
When man's work is done.

5 Work, for the night is coming ;
Work through the sunny noon ;
Fill brightest hours with labor ;
Rest comes sure and soon.
Give every flying minute
Something to keep in store ;
Work, for the night is coming
When man works no more.

3 Work, for the night is coming,
Under the sunset skies ;
While their bright tints are glowing,
Work, for daylight flies.
Work, till the last beam fadeth,
Fadeth to shine no more ;
Work, while the night is dark'ning,
When man's work is o'er.

Indexes.

→✳TITLES.✳←

110

➤❄FIRST✦LINES.❄◄

J. M. Armstrong & Co., Music Typographers, Philadelphia.

www.ingramcontent.com/pod-product-compliance
Lightning Source LLC
Chambersburg PA
CBHW032113010726
47493CB00008B/2562